CHRISTMAS FLINGS AND WEDDING RINGS

LITTLE BAMTON BOOK 5

BETH RAIN

CHAPTER 1

LUCY

'*H*ow're you doing back there?' Caro's voice sounded slightly muffled through the thick red curtain of the changing room. Lucy sighed. She wasn't sure she was quite ready to face her friends yet. She raised her hand and gently stroked the white velvet that fell in soft folds across her chest in a sweeping cowl neck that tumbled from twisted plaits that formed the halter straps of the dress.

'Erm . . .' she said, playing for time. She could almost feel Caro's raised eyebrows and Eve's look of concern from the other side of the curtain.

Lucy let out a sigh. She'd fallen in love with this dress the minute Caro had first shown it to her. The moment she set eyes on it, she'd been able to imagine herself walking down the aisle in the library at Bamton Hall. Walking towards her beautiful Sue and the rest of their life together.

But now that she was in here, trying it on at last . . . well, she didn't know if she could face the heartbreak if it didn't suit her. What if it didn't?! She was pretty curvy, after all. Maybe she was an idiot for falling for it in the first place. Caro had promised her that she'd be able to make any alterations necessary, but what if it wasn't right - just like the dozens if not hundreds of dresses she'd already tried on?

She simply couldn't bring herself to look in the mirror.

The dress certainly *felt* like it fit her well - the heavy, snowy velvet with its gentle crushed pattern of snowflakes and vines that curved sinuously up the full skirt had fallen with a luxurious whisper down over her curves. It was really long - the hem fell way lower than it needed to - the skirt pooling around her feet, and the little train at the back was currently more of a trip hazard than an elegant addition - but then, she'd have heels on when the big day came. Or she *would* if she ever got around to buying some.

She'd need to get the girls to help her out with the long line of little buttons up the back - and until she manned up and stepped out of here, she wouldn't have a clue if this was going to work or not.

'Lucy,' Eve's gentle voice was the next to greet her, 'you know we're here to help you, right?'

'I know,' said Lucy with a gusty sigh. 'I just . . . I'm not sure . . .'

'Sweetheart,' said Caro, 'it's your wedding dress. If

you're not sure, then we need to sort it out. Let me help! It's why we're doing this, right?'

'I guess. You're right. Sorry . . . I just want everything to be perfect.'

'It will be - I promise,' said Caro, 'but you're going to have to let us see you at some point!'

Lucy sucked in a deep breath. See, this was the problem with living in a tiny village. This wasn't anonymous in the slightest. If she'd have snuck off on her own to another town, she could be as neurotic as she wanted and no one who mattered would have been any the wiser. But she wasn't. She was in Caro's little vintage shop in the craft centre, being an idiot in front of two of her best friends. On top of that, anyone could be walking past the windows.

'I don't want anyone else to see me . . . in case . . .'

'No problem,' came Caro's voice. 'I mean, everyone else has pretty much closed up for the night anyway, but we'll shift a couple of clothes racks across the centre of the shop to block the view.'

Lucy heard a load of trundling and grumbling, and she guiltily turned and twisted in the dress trying to make sure that it was sitting straight. She'd managed to mostly cover the long mirror by draping it with her jeans and jumper, but towards the bottom, she caught a tantalising glimpse of snowy velvet and caught her breath. This *had* to be her dress!

'Alright lovely,' said Caro, 'you're safe to come out.'

Lucy took another deep breath, gathered the long

skirt in her hands and pushed her way through the gap in the curtain.

Eve and Caro were perched on a couple of high stools they'd brought over from Eve's art studio earlier, and Lucy felt like she could barely meet their eyes. She didn't want to see the disappointment in them, so she stared fixedly at the floor as she dropped the skirt and smoothed the fabric down with shaking fingers.

'Oh my . . .'

Lucy glanced at Caro just in time to see her hand fly to her mouth. She looked like she was going to cry.

'Luce!' breathed Eve. Then she paused and frowned. 'Why do you look so miserable?' she demanded. 'Don't you like it?'

Lucy shrugged. 'I don't know.'

'How can you not know?' squeaked Caro, dabbing at her eyes quickly with a tissue. 'You look like a . . . a . . .'

'Mess?' said Lucy.

'How can you even say that?' asked Eve.

'Goddess. You look like a goddess,' said Caro.

'Oh hush!' said Lucy. Her heart felt like it was in her mouth and she was fighting to stop herself from wiping her sweaty palms down the length of the skirt.

This was ridiculous! She wasn't this neurotic, clothes-obsessed nutter! She was the landlady to the village pub for heaven's sakes. She pulled pints whilst wearing her chunky knits, oversized men's shirts and cord dungarees. Why on earth was this so damned important?

That was an easy answer - because she'd never, ever expected this to happen. After so many disastrous dates and false starts, she'd somehow made peace with the idea of going through life without her soul mate by her side. Sure, she was surrounded by wonderful friends, but she'd never had that lightning-strike moment. Or at least, she hadn't until last Christmas, when she'd turned to Sue and instead of finding her best friend looking back at her, she'd found the love of her life.

'Do you really not like it?' asked Eve, bringing her crashing back into the moment.

'I *really* don't know,' said Lucy with a rueful smile. 'I haven't actually looked yet.'

'*What?!*' yelped Caro, manoeuvring herself carefully down off her stool, her hand resting unconsciously on the little baby bump that was just about visible underneath her voluminous pinafore dress. At around five months, it was proving to be one of the neatest bumps Lucy had ever seen.

Lucy quickly held up her hands in a gesture of surrender. 'Sorry, but I couldn't face it looking awful. I love this dress. I did the second you showed it to me . . . but . . . what if it doesn't love me?!'

'I promise you - it does!' said Eve, sounding almost desperate to convince her.

'Come here,' laughed Caro, gently angling Lucy so that she could work her way up the line of tiny, covered buttons at the back. 'Oh, there's one missing. No worries though, I can easily do something about that.'

Lucy felt the loose swathes of material draw in around her, and she practically stopped breathing as she waited for the final verdict.

'Okay, what size shoe are you?' asked Caro briskly.

'Six,' said Lucy. Her heart was now hammering. She was pretty sure that the entire village would be able to hear it by this point.

'Oh good!' said Caro, 'that's nice and easy!'

She headed straight for one of the old wooden drawers that she'd hung on brackets from the walls, and lifted down a pair of shimmering, silver heels.

'Not quite my style,' giggled Lucy nervously.

'I know,' said Caro, smiling at her, 'but you can slip them on to see how heels will look . . . unless you were planning on wearing your knackered old converse?' she added, raising an eyebrow.

Lucy shook her head. 'Nope. As much as that's a very tempting plan - I need the height, otherwise I might have considered it. There's this pair of amazing shoes I've had my eyes on but I didn't want to order them until I had the dress . . . you know, just in case they didn't go together. Maybe I've left it too late . . . I'm just not sure they'll arrive in time.' She paused and sighed. 'I can't believe I left this all so late.'

Caro placed the silver shoes in front of her and as

Lucy slid her bare feet into them, Eve dashed over and grabbed her hand for support.

'Stop stressing, lovely. You were waiting for the right dress,' said Eve with a shrug. 'We'll get it all sorted out, don't worry.'

Lucy nodded. The three of them - joined by both Emmy and Amber at times - had trekked to Exeter and Plymouth, and when that hadn't worked out they'd started driving even further afield. They'd trawled the wedding dress shops, braved the snooty assistants, guzzled the free champers and generally had a great time . . . but Lucy simply hadn't found the dress of her dreams. Every single time she'd tried one on, she'd felt like she was a kid playing dress-up. Then Caro had come back triumphant from a huge vintage sale with an entire car-full of new stock for her shop . . . and this dress.

'Okay,' said Eve. 'Time to Lucy-up!'

'Eh?' laughed Lucy.

'Close your eyes, it's time for you to get a proper look at yourself.'

Caro took hold of her hand and Lucy obediently closed her eyes, doing her best not to hyperventilate while trying to keep her balance on the unfamiliar shoes.

'Two secs,' said Eve, sounding a bit out of breath. 'Keep 'em closed. Annnnnnd . . . open!'

Lucy opened her eyes and went completely still.

Eve had dragged the full-length mirror out of the

changing room and was holding it up in front of her. There was no getting away from it now. She was face to face with herself.

Lucy blinked a couple of times, trying to take it all in. She still looked like herself, but . . . more so, somehow. All the other dresses she'd tried had looked like they were wearing her, rather than the other way around, but this one was different.

'Well?' said Caro, watching her in the mirror.

'It fits!' said Lucy, incredulously. 'Well, mostly,' she added with a grin, plucking at the bust. There was a bit of loose fabric going on at the sides under her arms.

'That's a really easy fix,' said Caro. 'And it won't take me any time to sort it out. I'll just need to pin it when you have the bra you're wearing for the wedding.'

'God,' groaned Lucy, 'don't tell me I need new undies too?!'

Eve giggled. 'I think most brides jump at the chance . . . but there aren't any rules!'

'Course there aren't,' said Caro, 'but you'll need a bra without straps - or maybe even a bodice type thing so that we get to see that amazing halter neck properly and plenty of cleavage under that cowl!' she grinned.

Lucy could feel herself going red, which was ridiculous. 'Do you think . . . that maybe it's a bit much?' she asked.

'No,' said Eve, a decisive note to her voice. 'It is exactly and perfectly the right amount of luscious-

Lucy-goodness. Seriously, you've got an amazing figure and this really shows it off.'

'It does!' said Caro, nodding enthusiastically, clearly having spotted her look of doubt. 'Look - if you're really uncomfortable with the amount of boobage on show, I could probably make some kind of modesty panel out of lace for you? It wouldn't block the shape of the neckline or hide your skin completely, but maybe make you feel a bit braver?'

Lucy stared hard at her reflection then shook her head. 'No - I actually like it the way it is.'

'Yay!' said Caro, bouncing on the balls of her feet in her excitement.

'So . . . is this the one?' asked Eve.

Lucy nodded, barely able to take her eyes off herself as both her friends squeezed her hands in excitement.

'Right. Looks like you'd better order those shoes!' said Caro. 'And . . . do you have a strapless bra that you want to wear?'

Lucy shook her head. 'Nope. I think you're right - I'm going to have to go shopping again, aren't I?!' she said with a groan.

Eve shook her head. 'Order a bunch online. Then you can try them all on with the dress and you'll know which one works best. And don't forget some matching knickers!'

'Don't you think my Bridget Jones style giant pants are going to work?' giggled Lucy.

Caro shook her head. 'You're impossible!'

CHAPTER 2

SUE

'*O*kay, pass me one more!' said Amber, reaching one hand down towards Sue whilst holding onto the top of the willow arch with the other and somehow maintaining her precarious balance on the old wooden stepladder while she was at it.

Sue quickly grabbed another withy from the fast dwindling pile on the library floor and handed it up to Amber before quickly placing a steadying hand on her friend's back as she wobbled.

'Steady on!' laughed Sue.

'You'd think I'd have the hang of this after all these years, wouldn't you?' grinned Amber, starting to weave the new withy deftly into the top of the archway.

'It's this ladder of Horace's,' said Sue, eyeballing it, 'it's not exactly sturdy, is it?!'

'I've clambered up worse!' said Amber, not taking her eyes off the job in hand.

Sue shook her head with a smile. Amber was basically afraid of nothing. She was probably one of the most fearless women she'd ever met - and ever since she'd got together with Will back in the Autumn, it was like her sense of daring, bouncy enthusiasm had blossomed even further. She had to face it - her friend was a total nutter.

Sue didn't have any regrets about asking Amber to be her maid of honour, but she had to admit that she was glad that Mark, Little Bamton's vicar and another one of her very best friends, had agreed to be her best man. At least that meant she was a little bit less likely to end up having to jump out of a plane on her hen do!

'Have you and Mark decided what we're going to do for my hen do yet?' asked Sue lightly, a little part of her hoping that if she managed to sneak this question in while Amber was distracted, she might actually manage to surprise an answer out of her.

'Nice try!' chuckled Amber, still not taking her eyes off what she was doing.

'Oh, come on. Mark won't tell me either!'

'No chance, Sue Taylor. It's a surprise.'

'Okay, fine. I just don't want to wake up naked and chained to a lamppost in Dublin, okay?'

'That is an oddly specific worry,' said Amber, finally pausing in what she was doing to peer down from the top of the ladder.

Sue shrugged. 'Happened to one of the guys at work on his stag do!'

'Poor bloke!' laughed Amber, climbing slowly back down to the safety of the library floor. 'Look, don't worry. I promise that you'll enjoy it and that we'll get you back to Little Bamton safe and sound in time for your big day, okay? And just for one last time, you're sure you don't want Lucy there?'

Sue shook her head. 'It's not that I don't want her there - I mean, it's going to be so weird *without* her there - we've been friends for soooo many years. But we both decided that we wouldn't go on each other's hen dos and that we'd have them on different nights as all our friends are basically the same people!'

Amber nodded. 'Okay. Just wanted to double-check.'

'Thanks!' Sue slung an arm around Amber's shoulders as they stood and surveyed her handiwork.

'What do you think?' asked Amber. 'Reckon Lucy will like the surprise?'

Sue nodded, looking at the amazing arched willow tunnel that now ran the length of the library from the doorway to where they would say their vows in front of the huge windows that overlooked the grounds. It was truly beautiful - and she could only imagine how stunning it would be when Emmy'd worked her flower magic on it too. The willow wove together to form great swirls and arcs. It felt like something straight out of a Tolkien novel.

'She's not going to believe it!' said Sue. 'The only trouble we're going to have is keeping her out of here until the big day - she's gone into planning panic overdrive!'

'Don't worry, we'll figure out how to keep her out until then,' laughed Amber, 'even if I have to set Diesel and Tarmac on guard duty.'

'Like those two would be any use!' laughed Sue. 'All she'd need was a rich tea biscuit and they'd be putty in her hands!'

'You might have a point there! But Lucy won't come up now though, will she? I mean, the wedding's only a week away . . .'

Sue shrugged. 'She might - just to quadruple check on everything. I've never seen her so worked up. Part of me thinks that maybe we'd have been better choosing to do this at quite literally any time of the year other than Christmas.'

'But surely the whole point is that Christmas is important to you both!' said Amber gently, turning to look at Sue properly.

Sue nodded. 'Yeah - I know. But Luce is so used to feeding the entire village and providing them with a communal living room all the way through to New Year that the whole wedding thing seems to have really thrown her into a tizzy. She's on a mission to make sure that she's not going to let anyone down for Christmas. I swear I've never seen a to-do list like it. It's more like a scroll!'

'Blimey,' said Amber with a frown. 'That's unlike Luce - she's usually so chilled. But hey - this is Little

Bamton. You've both got the whole village to lean on. All Lucy just needs to do is whisper that she needs help and she'll be inundated!'

Sue chuckled darkly. 'Ah well, there you have it, you've hit the nail on the head - my wife-to-be is the most amazing person I know - but not so hot when it comes to *asking for help*.'

Amber rolled her eyes. 'Okay, you may have a point.'

'Yeah,' sighed Sue. 'I mean, even with Caro's determination and clothes obsession - she hasn't managed to get Lucy to even buy her own wedding dress yet!'

'Not what I heard!' replied Amber in a sing-song voice, turning to tuck in a stray end of willow on one of the swirls.

'*What?!*' said Sue in surprise. 'Don't tell me there have been developments?!'

'Didn't Lucy tell you?' said Amber in surprise.

Sue shook her head. 'Nope. I was beginning to imagine her drifting down the aisle towards me wearing dungarees, wellies and a headscarf!' she laughed. 'Not that it would bother me - Luce looks beautiful in quite literally everything-'

'Awww you soppy mare!' laughed Amber, turning to grin at her.

Sue batted her playfully on the arm. 'You know what I mean,' she huffed. 'I just really want her to pamper herself and remember to actually *enjoy her own wedding!*' said Sue. 'Plus, if Lucy's dressing down, I'm sooo up for wearing my jeans!'

'Well, tough luck on that front old girl,' said Amber, linking arms with her and leading her towards the door, 'sounds like Luce is going to go full-on glamour-puss after all - so you'd better not let the side down!'

'As if I would!' said Sue with a grin. 'Anyway, my niece has been practising my hairdo for the big day on her friends for weeks,' she said, flipping her long grey plat over her back out of the way. 'I don't think she'd forgive me if I told her I was doing a *dress down* wedding! You know, I don't think I've ever talked about clothes and hair and all this stuff so much in my entire life!' she said, as they left the beautiful library behind them and headed towards the door that led back out into Bamton Hall's grounds.

'Sounds like you need an antidote to all things girly?' said Amber.

Sue nodded with a sigh. 'Hell yes!'

'Good, I was hoping you'd say that. There's a massive patch of brambles at the side of my willow bed I could do with a hand in clearing.'

'You're unbelievable,' laughed Sue, shaking her head. 'But yay!' she added. 'Let me just grab my overalls and gloves from the truck!'

'Wow, you two!' laughed Will coming to a halt at the open gateway into Amber's willow bed and raising his eyebrows. 'What's brought all this on?'

'Hey Will!' grinned Sue, turning to greet Amber's other half as he eyeballed the massive pile of hacked-down brambles, obviously impressed by the amount of work the pair of them had managed to achieve. She took a step towards him, only to get bulldozed by two over-excited chocolate Labradors as they dashed towards her. Sue promptly wobbled in her wellies and would have toppled over backwards into the mud if it hadn't been for Amber's steadying hand on her shoulder.

'Sit!' said Amber sharply from behind her.

Sue chuckled as Diesel and Tarmac planted their behinds into the grass and watched her friend with adoring eyes.

'Do you feel like you should sit too, every time she does that?' Sue grinned at Will.

'Every single time,' he laughed, 'I probably would if I liked treats as much as those two,' he added, nodding at the dogs who were now busily snaffling the stinky treats that had magically appeared from Amber's pocket.

'I'll bear that in mind!' said Amber, before sticking her tongue out at Will.

'Now then, that's no way to treat your boss,' said Sue.

'Oh, don't you worry, I'm under no illusions about being anything of the sort,' said Will, throwing his arm around Amber's shoulders as she came to stand with him. 'Anyway - what *did* bring on this sudden urge to clear brambles? I thought you two were getting the library all wedding-ready . . .'

'Been there and done that,' said Sue. 'It looks beautiful thanks to Amber's magic hands. But . . . I needed something practical to get my teeth into.'

'Yeah,' said Amber, 'Sue's all bridaled out!'

'So you thought you'd take advantage of an extra pair of hands for some heavy lifting?' chuckled Will.

Amber shrugged. 'I see it as pre-wedding therapy.'

'Just don't expect all our brides to want to end their days digging bramble prickles out of their hands!' laughed Will, watching as Sue removed a particularly stubborn one from her thumb as the dogs bounded around her.

'Yeah Amber,' Sue muttered, 'I'm one of a kind!'

'As If I could ever forget it!' laughed Amber. 'So - did you need me?' she added, turning to Will.

'Always,' he said with a cheesy grin.

'Awwwww!' said Sue, giving up on a second prickle and ruffling Tarmac's ears instead. 'You guys! Quit being so disgustingly cute.'

'Yeah Will,' said Amber with a grin as he turned pink. 'Sue needs a break from the mushy stuff.'

'Really?' he said in surprise.

'Nah. Not really,' Sue said with a soppy smile of her own.

'Oh good - because Finn's just arrived to help you with your vows!'

'Balls,' said Sue. She'd forgotten she'd arranged to

meet Finn. She'd been having so much fun helping Amber tame the little wilderness that was her pride and joy, she'd forgotten how much she was dreading this part of the day.

'Hey,' said Amber, raising her eyebrows as they set off back towards the Hall, 'what's up?'

'It's me and words,' said Sue. 'We don't get on.'

'Ha, you and me both,' chuckled Amber. 'You know how crap I am with saying things in the right way.'

'I think that's why we get on so well!' said Sue. 'But luckily for you, you don't have to stand up in front of your family and the entire bloody village and declare your undying love to someone who's changed your entire life.'

'Oh my god,' said Will, nudging her arm, 'just say that and they'll all bawl their eyes out!'

'Excellent,' said Sue, her face deadpan. 'Job done. Can I go home now?'

'Ah come on,' said Amber, 'it won't be that bad! Finn will help you get it right - and anyway, he's that excited about it, you wouldn't want to disappoint the poor lad, would you?'

Sue shrugged. 'I guess,' she muttered. 'But there'd better be some decent homebrew on offer to get me through it, that's all I'm saying!'

CHAPTER 3

LUCY

Flowers - still to do.
        Shoes - on their way.
Dress - done. Alterations underway.
Sprouts - must talk to Alf
Ring - to collect! God, I hope she likes it...
Tree - Sam sponsoring again.
Lights - must talk to Mark re: tree lighting ceremony
Vows -

'Balls!'

'Luce, you okay?' asked Emmy, peering at her friend from her perch on the other side of the bar.

'Sure. Of course. Why?' said Lucy, distractedly polishing the pint glass in her hand with a checked tea towel.

'Well . . . you've been polishing the same glass for nearly five minutes, you're muttering under your breath and staring into the middle distance, and you just said "balls" to Violet!' said Emmy, casting a sideways glance at Violet who was still standing next to her, looking mildly scandalised.

'Violet! Oh my . . . I'm so sorry!' said Lucy.

'Don't you worry dear,' said Violet with a small smile. 'But a sherry when you've finished that conversation with yourself would be wonderful!'

'Of course!' said Lucy, quickly putting down the glass and the tea towel and turning to pour Violet's drink for her.

She took a deep breath, making the most of a couple of seconds of relative privacy while she had her back to the rest of the room. She *had* to pull herself together. The pub was mega-busy for a random Wednesday evening, and she was manning the bar on her own. She really *really* needed to stop obsessing over her to-do list while she was working, otherwise she was going to go completely nuts - not to mention she didn't really want to upset the entire village while she was at it. Or have them think she was barmy, come to that!

'Here we go!' she said, plastering a smile on her face and handing Violet her drink. 'On the house, Vi. Is Horace with you? Does he want his usual?'

'Oh, erm . . . no,' said Violet shiftily. 'I'm just waiting for . . .'

Lucy caught a swift movement out of the corner of her eye. It looked as though Emmy had just nudged Violet in the ribs with her elbow. What one earth?!

'I mean . . . I'm . . . just me,' Violet finished, looking flustered.

'Okay. Well, enjoy!' said Lucy.

Violet hurried off to her favourite perch over by the fireplace, and Lucy turned and stared hard at Emmy. Something weird was definitely afoot. 'What was all that about?'

'You probably threw her for a loop by acting like a nutter,' said Emmy with a grin.

Lucy rolled her eyes. 'Was it that bad?'

'Bad? No! Funny? Yes!' chuckled Emmy.

'Jeez, thanks,' sighed Lucy.

'Seriously though, are you okay?'

Lucy nodded, catching the look of genuine concern on her friend's face, and then she shrugged. 'There's just a lot to do and I'm dreading forgetting something - with the wedding and Christmas and . . .'

'And?' prompted Emmy, raising her eyebrows.

'Oh, nothing,' sighed Lucy. 'I'm just a bit nervous, I guess. I could do with a night off thinking about the whole thing - it's taking over everything.'

'A night out you say?' said Emmy, waggling her eyebrows.

'No, Em,' laughed Lucy, 'I said a night off . . . not out!'

'Well, close enough,' she said with a grin.

'Emmy Martin, what are you up to?' demanded Lucy, eyeing her friend, who suddenly seemed to have a suspicious twinkle in her eye.

'Oh . . . it's not just Emmy!'

'Eve! Hi!' said Lucy, beaming at her as she materialised seemingly out of nowhere.

'No, definitely *not* just Emmy,' said Caro, appearing at Lucy's side behind the bar.

'What are *you* doing here?' said Lucy, turning to Caro. 'You're not due to work tonight!'

'Nope, she's not,' said Sue, popping up next to Caro. 'That's what I'm here for!'

'Eh?' said Lucy, now completely confused, but leaning into Sue's kiss on her cheek with a contented sigh.

'We're kidnapping you,' said Caro, holding up a hand and dangling a black, silk blindfold in front of her.

'No you're not!' laughed Lucy, unable to keep the hint of nerves out of her voice as a swoop of excitement ran through her.

'Oh yes they are!' laughed Sue.

'But I'm working,' said Lucy, 'and I've got too much to do, and-'

'And nothing!' said Sue, tucking a stray curl behind Lucy's ear. 'Time for you to relax and have a bit of fun. Don't worry - I'm here to cover this place and I think Sam's going to pop down a bit later too?' she added peeping at Caro, who gave her the thumbs up.

'You sure?' said Lucy.

'Of course. Now go!' said Sue, giving her a last kiss, making Lucy's toes curl in delight. But it was over far too soon, and Sue manoeuvred her towards Caro, who quickly threw a sparkly sash over her shoulders and then pulled the blindfold over her eyes before she could protest.

Lucy couldn't help the grin of excitement that spread over her face, even as she felt Caro's hands grab both of hers and tug her forwards to lead her from behind the bar.

'Bring her back in one piece, won't you?!' she heard Sue call with a laugh, as what sounded like everyone else in the pub started cheering and clapping.

Lucy suddenly became very aware that she was only wearing a short-sleeved denim shirt and a pair of ripped jeans as she felt the temperature drop drastically. The freezing December breeze tickled her arms and she guessed Caro must have just trouped her out of the front door of the pub- though where on earth these mad blighters thought they were going to take her was anyone's guess. Maybe they'd set up something over in the craft centre . . .

'You know,' said a voice Lucy recognised but couldn't quite place, 'it *does* seem a bit of a shame to bundle her in there without her getting to see it!'

'She's right! Take it off!' said Violet, so close to her ear that it made her jump.

Lucy felt someone fumbling with the knot on her blindfold and suddenly she found herself facing the most ridiculous car she'd ever set eyes on.

'Holy moly,' she laughed.

She was staring at a bubble-gum pink stretch Limo. Somehow, Lucy highly doubted such a beast had ever graced Little Bamton's village square before. Frankly, the driver must be a total lunatic for even thinking that navigating the narrow lanes into the village in this monster was a good idea. She shuddered to think how he'd managed to get over the double humpback bridge without stranding himself.

'How . . . where . . .?' she stuttered looking around at the excited gang around her. There was Violet, grinning at her with a little glass of sherry still clutched in her hands, and next to her was Scarlet - who'd recently started to help her out on Saturdays after Eve had introduced them. Then, of course, there was Eve herself, Emmy, Caro and . . .

'Where's Amber?!' she asked. Clearly, she was being kidnapped for her hen do, and it was bad enough that Sue wasn't going to be there - there was no way she was going without the sixth and final member of the Little Bamton book club!

'Right here checking out the facilities!' laughed Amber, her face appearing as she rolled down the back window of the ridiculous car, waggling a bottle of champagne at them all. 'Come on you lot - it's adventure time!'

The suited and be-capped chauffeur grinned at them and opened the door as Caro ushered Lucy forwards.

'This is totally nuts,' giggled Lucy, settling herself

onto the squashy leather seat and eyeballing the fairy lights, mistletoe and tinsel that clashed delightfully with the flashes of bubble-gum pink here and there. 'Where are we going?' she asked.

'We're not going to tell you that easily,' laughed Scarlet, rolling her eyes.

'But . . . I'm a state!' said Lucy, plucking at her shirt, and then looking the others up and down with mounting panic. 'You all look absolutely stunning!'

'This old thing?' laughed Amber, smoothing down the little black velvet number she was wearing.

'Oh give over!' chuckled Caro and elbowing Amber in the ribs. 'This is the first time I've ever seen you in a dress!'

'Me too,' said Eve.

'Me three,' nodded Emmy.

'I like it,' said Scarlet.

'Thanks,' grinned Amber. 'Actually, so did Will. Didn't think he was going to let me leave the hall for a moment there!'

'Eew!' said Scarlet, with a look that only a super-cool and slightly grossed-out teenager can pull off.

Lucy let out a snort. 'You do look amazing. And I'm just . . .'

'Don't worry about that,' said Caro, grabbing her hand to steady herself as the driver set off, turning the massive vehicle in what felt like a nine-hundred point turn to get it back out of the square.

'How can I not worry . . . I smell of pub!'

'Sue's packed you something pretty. You'll get the chance to change when we get there.'

'Where?' said Lucy quickly.

'Nice try, Lucy Brown,' laughed Amber.

'Alright my loves,' said Emmy, grabbing the bottle of chilled champagne from Amber, 'time for a toast!' She popped the cork and poured out a glass for all of them before handing them around, and then passing an elderflower fizz to Caro.

Lucy raised her glass with the rest of them, her heart hammering with nerves and excitement. She had no idea where they were going, but she knew she loved this little group of friends with a kind of fierce intensity that took her breath away.

'To Lucy and Sue,' said Amber. 'And true love, and . . .'

'And friendship,' added Violet.

'And champagne!' said Scarlet.

They all cheered and took a sip of their drinks, doing their best not to inhale the bubbles as the driver took the humpback bridge at surprising speed.

'Ooh! Christmas tunes,' said Lucy with a sigh, as Bing Crosby started crooning. 'Girls, thank you for this . . . whatever *this* is,' she said grinning around at them all.

'It's going to be sooo much fun,' said Scarlet, bouncing slightly in her chair. 'We need selfies!' she said yanking her phone out of the pocket of her leather jacket. 'Ooh . . . two secs . . .'

Lucy watched as Scarlet peered at the screen, went an interesting shade of pink and quickly started to type something.

'I know that look,' said Emmy with a naughty smile. 'Who's messaging you, missus?!'

'No one,' she said, then looking up to find them all staring at her avidly, she rolled her eyes. 'Okay, fine. It's Davy.'

'Davy?' gasped Eve, 'as in, my Davy?!'

Scarlet nodded. 'Yeah - he just messaged me to say Finn's back from London.'

'But why'd he tell you, not me?' said Eve.

'Erm . . . apparently your phone's still on the kitchen table?'

Lucy laughed as she watched Eve pat her pockets with a look of confusion on her face.

'Oh. Right,' said Eve looking mildly sheepish.

'Typical Eve,' said Caro with a grin. 'You and your phone don't have a very close relationship, do you?!'

Eve shrugged. 'Nope. And life is sooooo much sweeter that way.'

'So,' said Amber, grinning at Scarlet, 'you and our Davy-boy, huh?!'

'Ah maaaan!' whined Scarlet, causing everyone to laugh. 'We're just friends, okay?!'

'Oh yes?' said Violet, wiggling her eyebrows at Scarlet, who sank back in her seat and closed her eyes as if that would make them all go away and leave her alone.

'Okay okay, we'll back off,' said Caro.

'Yeah,' said Lucy, patting the young girl on the shoulder. 'It's only because we're all jealous. Paired off, romance behind us . . .'

Scarlet opened her eyes and raised a sceptical eyebrow at Lucy. 'You're about to get married to the love of your life,' she said. 'It doesn't get much more romantic than that.'

This made everyone let out a round of cheers, and Lucy felt the heat rush to her face.

'I'm so glad Finn's back,' sighed Eve. 'I was imagining a snowfall like last year and him getting stranded in London and missing the wedding and Christmas and everything!'

'Didn't he just nip up there for one night?' laughed Violet.

'Okay, yeah, fine. So I've got an overactive imagination,' said Eve. 'It comes from living with a famous author! I barely feel like I've spent any time with him recently. He's been in full-on first draft mode - wandering around in a daze when he's not attached to the typewriter. He's taken to talking to his imaginary friends again,' she smirked.

Violet spluttered. 'That can't be a good sign!'

'Oh - it is . . . it usually means it's going well.'

'So,' asked Lucy, sending a sneaky glance at Scarlet, 'how is it having Davy home?'

'Erm – really weird, if I'm honest,' said Eve.

'Uh oh,' said Emmy, 'that sounds a bit ominous.'

'No,' said Eve, shaking her head quickly and

swirling the dregs of the champagne around her glass, 'that's just it, it's not weird at all. I thought there'd be some teething issues with him being in the same space as Finn for the first time, but they seem to adore each other!'

'Surely that's a good thing?' laughed Caro.

'Definitely,' said Eve, 'but it means I spent weeks worrying about the whole thing for nothing. I was so worried. I mean – I really needed Davy to feel like it was still the home he's always known.'

'That's really sweet,' said Scarlet quietly.

'Well, I've not lived with a bloke since Davy's dad left when he was just two. He's never even known me to date anyone, so I was-'

'Shitting yourself?' said Caro delicately.

'You could say that!' laughed Eve. 'But Davy seems to be loving it. I mean, you should see him with Wilf. I swear that dog's barely left his side!'

'Traitorous hound,' laughed Scarlet, who walked Wilf several times a week, especially when Finn was away.

'I think it's cute!' said Emmy. 'And how's Finn doing with it all?'

'You know Finn – he's half in a world of his own making a lot of the time – and he's been on this deadline so I thought he'd find it difficult – but he's loving it too. He disappears into his office as usual, gets his word count done for the day and then as soon as he reappears, Davy's got him into some computer game and they spend more time together on that than anything else.'

'Tell me about it,' said Scarlet. 'They've got a total bromance going on. I'm actually chuffed Finn had to go to London - I got to actually see Davy earlier!' she grinned.

'Are you two dating then?' said Violet with interest.

Scarlet shrugged. 'We've been chatting while he's been away at uni, that's all.'

'Ooooh chatting, eh?' said Amber.

'I thought you were going to drop it?' muttered Scarlet.

'You brought it back up.'

'You *fancy* him!' said Amber. 'Davy and Scarlet sitting in a tree, K. I. S. S. I-'

'What are you, two years old?' chuckled Lucy, prodding Amber with her foot.

'I'd say about six - and proud of it,' grinned Amber, winking at Scarlet who grinned back.

'Eve - I'm so glad the boys are getting on,' said Lucy. 'I know how worried you were!'

'Yeah,' laughed Eve, 'and now I feel like a complete idiot. Families, eh?! I swear I keep pinching myself – it feels too good to be true.'

'You've been saying that ever since you and Finn got together,' laughed Caro. 'How about you, Luce – any worries about Sue's family?'

Lucy smiled and shrugged. 'Not really. We've been

friends for years, so I know them all pretty well. Of course, neither of her parents are alive, but her brothers and sister have even stayed with me before, and the kids - all her nephews and nieces - seem to be taking the change of circumstances in their stride. As in – I don't think they really realise anything's changed at all!'

'That's pretty perfect then,' said Eve.

Lucy nodded. 'I just wish Sue's parents were still with us. I mean, out of all of them, it's just my lovely mum left. I think she's doing her best to count for all four parents!'

'Aw!' said Caro. 'Hey – tell Sue she can borrow my parents.'

Lucy laughed. 'Ah, those two are pretty much honorary villagers by this point, aren't they? I mean, they're coming to the Christmas Eve carol service, aren't they?'

Caro nodded. 'They can't wait. Actually, I meant to ask – what are you going to do about the pub over Christmas? It'll be so weird not having lunch there - I loved last year so much.'

'Aren't you coming?' said Lucy, feeling a pang of sadness hit her squarely in the chest. After all, it was while she'd been tackling last year's sprout mountain with Caro and Sue she'd realised that her new feelings for her old friend weren't about to go away any time soon. Caro was a huge part of that moment - having just crash-landed into the village. She'd been there - an unwitting witness to the very start of their relationship.

'Well . . . I just assumed you'd be closed for a few weeks,' said Caro in surprise.

'Why?' said Lucy.

'Erm – honeymoon?' said Eve, raising her eyebrows.

'Yes - lots of naughty times for the new Mrs and Mrs!' said Amber, wiggling her eyebrows.

'Yes - I thought so too,' said Violet. 'In fact, I'm sure it was someone at the WI who told me you'd be closed, even though I'd already assumed that would be the case.'

'Oh no, do you think everyone else thinks the same thing?' said Lucy, her heart sinking.

'It's a fair bet . . . but it's not a big deal, is it? I mean, you *will* be away, won't you?' said Emmy.

Lucy shook her head looking desperate. 'No chance! We're getting married on the twenty-third so that all the Christmassy goodness Little Bamton has to offer will be like a looooong after-party! Complete with full Christmas dinner in the pub!'

'Don't panic,' said Eve gently. 'We'll all help you get the word out that Christmas dinner is still on! Maybe a little bit of advertising and some leaflets too . . .'

'Bugger,' breathed Lucy. 'I've been so focused on all the bits that *had* to be done to make sure that the wedding happens and that everything is ready for

Christmas day too, I didn't even think about letting everyone know that it's business as usual!'

'So you're not going away at all?' said Emmy in surprise.

'We will,' shrugged Lucy, 'but not until the summer. I mean, when you live in somewhere like Little Bamton . . .'

'You never really want to leave?' said Caro, gently rubbing her stomach with a smile.

'Precisely.'

'Right!' said Amber, 'time for a top-up ladies!' she said, precariously pouring more bubbly for them all.

'Alright for some!' muttered Caro, accepting another elderflower fizz from Amber once she'd done with the champagne.

'Sorry lovely,' said Amber.

'Don't you worry!' laughed Caro slinging an arm around Lucy. 'I was only joking. Well, mostly . . . though I'd love nothing more than a large glass of red, and some super ripe cheese . . . and everything else I'm not actually allowed right now.'

'Ah,' said Violet, raising her eyebrows, 'It's got to that stage, has it?'

Caro snorted out a laugh. 'Oh yes. I'm slowly but surely driving Sam potty! At this rate, he's going to chuck me out of the cabin and I'll be back living above the pub!'

'Well . . . it *is* still empty . . .' said Lucy with a grin.

'God, don't tell Sam that, will you? You might put the idea in his head!'

'No chance,' laughed Eve. 'That man adores you – I don't think I've ever seen him so excited about anything before. Did you know that every time he mentions the baby to any of the lads, he calls it "my apprentice"?'

'Aaw!' sighed Scarlet, 'that is *so* adorable!'

'Oh, I know,' grinned Caro. 'He's already presented me with baby-grows and a blanket that he's had embroidered with the words "Daddy's Little Apprentice." To be honest, he's been amazing. I'm just scared stiff I'm going to frighten him off with all the crazy hormone stuff!'

'Don't!' squeaked Lucy. 'I'm scared I'm going to do the same thing with Sue – and I don't even have the hormones to blame!'

'Same thing goes for Sue as for Sam,' said Eve.

'What,' giggled Emmy, 'has she ordered Luce a onesie with "My Little Apprentice" on it?'

Lucy snorted. 'Now there's a gift I'd appreciate!'

'No,' tutted Eve, 'I *meant* that I've never seen Sue so happy either. Ever since you two have been together, she's just been floating.'

Amber nodded. 'Eve's right. She's a smitten kitten.'

'Aw, you guys!' sighed Lucy, unable to stop the huge smile from spreading over her face, before it dropped again. 'But – what if I *do* turn into bridezilla? All this is so far out of my comfort zone - I'm turning into a total nightmare. I mean – just look at the palaver with the dress. Sue's going to end up hating me and…'

'Steady now,' said Violet gently, leaning forward slightly. 'This is you and Sue. This is Little Bamton. The whole village adores the pair of you and we'll do *anything* to make sure that your wedding is exactly how you want it to be.'

Scarlet nodded and patted Violet on the arm approvingly. 'Exactly. And besides - your version of Bridezilla would count as, I dunno - like - most people's best behaviour!'

'I just don't want to be a bother. And with Christmas just two days after the wedding-'

'This is going to be the best Christmas we've ever seen,' said Eve.

'Well, maybe apart from last year,' said Caro, 'but that one was pretty special, wasn't it?'

'You could say that again,' sighed Lucy as the smile spread over her face again. She couldn't think about last Christmas without reliving the moment she'd fallen in love with Sue.

'Oooh!' squealed Amber, turning to peer out of the darkened Limo window. 'Time to get that blindfold back in place, Luce - I think we're here!'

'Yeah, come on, you love-sick fool,' said Caro, 'time to stop fretting and have a bit of fun!'

CHAPTER 4

SUE

'Okay - all clear, they're gone!' called Lyndon from his perch next to one of the pub's front windows.

'Excellent,' beamed Sue. She grabbed an empty pint glass and a pen from under the bar and clanged her makeshift bell until she'd got everyone's attention. 'Alright you lot,' she called, 'most of you know what's happening in here this evening, but for anyone that doesn't - we're on a decorating mission. We'd normally do this when the pub's closed, but my lovely bride-to-be is getting herself in a tizzy with the wedding coming up, so we're taking this job off her hands, and while we're busy out here, the good ladies of the WI are going to take over the kitchens and magic up as many mince-pies as they can muster!

'Given that Lucy's just been kidnapped for her hen-do - this is our chance! Sorry if you were planning on a quiet drink - things might get a bit hectic, but the next round of drinks is on me - for the inconvenience and for your help!'

There was a round of cheers and Sue gave everyone a thumbs up before grabbing her mobile and quickly pulling up Sam's number.

'The hens have left the building. Repeat - the hens have left the building!' she said as soon as he picked up.

'Got it. We'll be right there!' said Sam.

Two minutes later, the pub door opened and a squat Christmas tree forced its way into the bar followed by Sam, who was practically buried in its branches.

'Over there, Sam!' said Sue, pointing to the opposite end of the room to where the fireplace sat. 'It'll drop fewer needles over there.'

'Isn't that one of those posh, non-drop jobbies anyway?' said Alf, who was next in line through the door, carrying a massive cardboard box in front of him. A hodgepodge of fake holly, tinsel and red ribbon stuck out the top of it.

'Yep,' said Sam, 'but it'll still fare a bit better away from the heat!'

'And I guess it won't catch fire like a couple of years ago,' chuckled Alf.

'Seriously?' said Finn, his eyes going wide as he hurried into the room and dashed over to set the wide metal stand he was carrying on the ground in front of Sam before helping him to guide the chunky stump of the tree into it. 'You seriously had a Christmas tree fire in here?'

'Alf's exaggerating,' chuckled Sue, easing her way out from behind the bar and rushing over to save Jon, who'd just wobbled his way through the door, carrying three boxes stacked so high that he couldn't see over the top of them. 'The tree just got a bit singed, that's all!' she added with a grunt as she lifted the top box down.

'But there was the delightful scent of freshly-barbe-cued pine tree in here for a few days!' laughed Sam, reappearing from behind the tree and squinting at it before giving it a yank to straighten it up as Finn did up the screws in the base.

'Well,' Jon, placing his remaining boxes onto the bar with a grunt of relief, 'that's got to be a good start – getting the tree in place without Lucy spotting you at it!'

Sue nodded. 'Thanks so much for agreeing to help, guys – I didn't mean for you to have to stay over in Sam's workshop for so long – the Limo driver was a bit later than expected.'

'I'm not surprised!' laughed Finn, 'can you imagine getting that thing over the bridge?'

'Anyway – it's all good – Caro made sure there was a ready supply of Guinness for us in my little fridge!' grinned Sam.

'Finn,' said Sue quickly, 'are you sure you're up for this? I know you've only just got back from London!'

'Of course!' he laughed. 'And Davy said he'll be over in a bit too.'

'I feel a bit bad for not inviting Horace,' said Sue with a sigh, 'but he tells Violet quite literally every-thing, and the pair of them are rubbish at keeping secrets!'

'Oh, don't worry about that,' said Sam. 'Will's on his way down with those willow stars you asked Amber to make for you and he's bringing Horace down with him.'

'So where's that pink monstrosity taking them all?' asked Lyndon, draining his pint and wandering over to join them. 'Looked to me like they were off to get good and messy!'

'Nah – probably quite sedate I reckon,' said Sue. 'They got me to put a pretty party dress in a bag for Luce – and her makeup – but they wouldn't tell me where they were off to!'

'*I* know,' said Sam, his eyes twinkling.

'Spill the beans then,' said Sue, raising her eyebrows.

'I guess it can't hurt now that she's on her way! There's a massive Christmas party over at the Upper Bamton vineyard – you know, the type where you buy a whole table?'

'Nice!' said Sue approvingly.

'Yeah – I'm jealous,' said Finn, grinning. 'I mean – wine tasting, loads of amazing food and then dancing.'

'I hope they have fun!' said Jon, smiling.

'From what I've seen, that's pretty much a dead cert

when the Little Bamton book club gets together,' said Sam.

'Gutted,' sighed Sue, 'it's the first meeting I've missed!'

'Well, they've got Scarlet and Violet there as honorary members to fill your place,' said Sam. 'Anyway – just you wait until your own do. Mark and Amber have been busy plotting!'

'Was that my name I just heard mentioned in vain?' came Mark's deep voice from the doorway.

Sue turned to see her best man ducking into the pub, followed by Will and Horace.

'Yep!' said Sam, clapping the vicar on the shoulder as he made his way over to them. 'Just telling Sue not to feel bad about missing out on Luce's hen-do as you and Amber have been busy plotting the perfect one for her.'

Mark nodded, and Will grinned. 'Amber's so excited!' he laughed.

'Amber's always excited,' chuckled Sue, shaking her head.

'Okay – you've got me there,' said Will, shrugging.

'So, what are you planning?' said Sue.

'I'm not telling,' laughed Mark, shooting Horace a quick look of warning as he opened his mouth, but he was too late.

'As long as you're free the day after tomorrow,' said Horace.

'Horace!' they all boomed – and he clamped his hand over his mouth in horror.

'Sorry, sorry, didn't you know that?' he spluttered.

Sue laughed and shook her head. 'Day after tomorrow, eh? No chance of you kidnapping me now is there?!'

'Aaaanyway!' breathed Sam, winking at Mark, 'hadn't we better get this place all decked with holly before the hens get back?'

Sue nodded. 'Yep – lots to do, but we've got all evening. They're not due back here before closing time, and I've got a feeling the girls will be pouring Luce straight back into her cottage when they're done with her!'

'Excellent,' said Mark, 'then we can be sure to have this place finished and looking amazing in time for it to be part of her hangover cure tomorrow. Now then Sue, where do you want us?'

Sue grinned at him. 'Well . . . Lyndon and Horace – can you two sort out the garlands for the beams? They're in those two boxes there - and then maybe rope in some of the other guys over there to help you put them up?' she added, pointing at a bunch of lads who were sitting with Lyndon's nephew.

Horace gave her the thumbs up, grabbed a box and disappeared to the corner table with Lyndon.

'Finn, Will – are you both up for sorting out the Christmas tree?'

'Gosh, I'm honoured,' said Finn with a smile, 'you sure you want the two new boys on the tree?'

'I'm sure!' laughed Sue. 'Lucy's usual instruction for

anyone helping with the tree is "go wild" – so … enjoy? Jon, did you bring your tools?'

Jon nodded. 'Just need to grab them from Sam's, I couldn't carry them as well as the boxes. But I'll get the bathroom sorted in no time!'

'Sorry,' said Sue, 'not exactly the most festive job!'

'If it's another thing off Lucy's to-do list, I'm happy to help!' Jon gave her a warm smile and headed back outside to fetch his bag.

'Mark,' said Sue, 'would you be up for manning the bar for a while?'

Mark nodded. 'Of course!'

'You know what you're doing, right?' she winked at him.

'I've been in this village long enough to know how to pull a pint,' he chuckled.

Sam grinned at him. 'Well, longer than Caro had before she was roped in last Christmas anyway – wasn't she on bar-duty on her second day here?'

Sue laughed. 'Yep. And she was hard at work on our sprout mountain from day one – after you'd spent a cosy first night together up at your cabin, of course!'

'Well,' said Sam, running his fingers through his hair awkwardly, 'didn't work out too badly for me in the end, did it?!'

'You're right there,' nodded Mark. 'A baby on the way …'

'My little apprentice!' beamed Sam.

'And an amazing woman to share your life with,' said Sue, suddenly feeling a bit teary.

'Hey!' said Sam, wrapping his arm around her shoulders. 'You okay?'

Sue smiled at him, swallowing the random lump of emotion that had suddenly swelled in her throat. 'I'm more than okay. Look at the incredible year we've had!'

'Well – it's not over yet,' said Mark with a smile. 'So – do you two want to test run my pint pulling prowess?' he waggled an empty pint glass at Sue.

'Oh, we will – but not yet. Sam and I have got something to do that's definitely a job to attempt *before* too many more pints!'

'You know the parish council are going to have your guts for garters, don't you?' puffed Sam.

'They can have what's left of me if I survive this!' said Sue, watching her breath plume in the cold air around her, even as she gripped the rung of the ladder she was half lying on top of. She didn't dare look down. Why oh why had she thought that this would be a fun plan?

'You okay there?' laughed Sam from somewhere behind her.

'Just taking a . . . breath!' she gulped.

'Sue . . . if you're afraid of heights, why on earth

didn't you rope one of the others into this hair-brained plan?!'

'I'm not afraid of heights!' said Sue sharply, still not able to unwrap her hand from the ladder rung.

'O-kay,' said Sam. 'So . . . you're just taking in the view?'

Sue would quite like to say something rude, but she was too busy trying to get her breathing under control. She wasn't afraid of heights. She was afraid of falling from them . . . and how much things would hurt if you *did* fall.

After all – maybe it *was* a spectacularly bad idea to be perched right at the top of a ladder, which in turn was perched right at the top of the flight of stone steps that ran up to the second floor of the back of the pub. If she turned her head, she'd be able to see right across the carpark to the fields that lay behind the pub. But she wasn't going to turn her head. She was too busy focusing on her white knuckles that were gripping the top rung of the ladder as if her life depended on it. Which it kind of did.

'Sam?'

'Yeah?'

'Would you mind swapping?'

'Sure,' he laughed.

Hm. It would be so easy to boot him in the face right now!

'Look,' said Sam, 'before we climb down, let me just

bung these onto the roof – it's one thing less to carry back up with me.'

'But . . . I can't let go,' said Sue, reluctantly.

'Okay – just hold on a sec.'

Sue closed her eyes and listened to the clonking below her. It sounded like Sam was getting closer. Then there was a thud just ahead of her, and she opened her eyes. There, on the edge of the roof, dangled a pair of booted legs wearing Santa trousers.

'Alright, let's go back down!' said Sam.

Ten minutes later, Sam had done the deed, and they both stood back down in the carpark of the pub, staring up at the rather bizarre sight of Santa disappearing headfirst down the pub's second, unused chimney stack.

'It looks amazing,' laughed Sue. 'Thank you!'

'Oh, no problem,' said Sam, grinning at her. 'There's nothing I like better than clambering around on a roof in the dark while cuddling a pair of Santa legs!'

Sue nudged him in the ribs with her elbow. 'Lucy's always wanted to do that – she's just never got around to giving it a try!'

'And now we know why!' laughed Sam.

Sue shrugged. 'All good – you've got yourself a job every Christmas now!'

'Oh yay, lucky me,' said Sam, smirking at her. 'Come on, I think we've earned that pint, don't you?

CHAPTER 5

LUCY

U *rgh.*
UUUURGH!

Lucy cracked one eye open. The sliver of light that flooded in was way too much to bear, so she clamped it shut again and tugged a blanket up over her head.

What the hell? Even that tiny movement caused a riot inside her head. It felt a bit like someone was stumbling around drunk in the percussion section of an orchestra. Was she ill? Maybe. Maybe that would explain why she felt like she was falling, even though she was lying down and had her eyes closed.

Yes. Clearly she was deathly ill. That was the only way to explain the fact that her mouth and throat had turned into sandpaper and her eyeballs felt like hot, crackling chestnuts inside her skull.

'Oh crap,' she muttered into the darkness under the blanket.

She sat up, then braced herself as the blanket fell away again. The entire room swayed and she fought the urge to leg it to the bathroom.

Where the hell was she? This wasn't her cosy bedroom in her cottage. It wasn't Sue's cottage either, come to that.

'What the hell am I doing up here?' she mumbled to herself, staring around the neat bedroom. She was in the little flat above the pub. She'd not lived here in . . . years.

Her eyes came to rest on a pint glass on the bedside table, full to the brim with water. Next to it, there was a blister pack of paracetamol and a lime-green post-it note. She reached over for the note and brought it close enough to her face that she could read it given that she didn't have her reading glasses with her.

Drink all the water. Take some pills. I'll be in to check on you in the morning. Caro x
P.S Epic dancing!

Epic dancing? Oh no! Oooooh no . . . no she wasn't ready to think about last night yet.

No.

Nope nope nope.

She was a grown woman. A mature, sensible

member of society! A . . . ah balls, who was she even trying to kid?

Lucy buried her face in her hands for a moment, willing the room to stop shifting around so much. She wracked her brain for the events of the previous evening. There had been dancing. A lot of dancing. And wine. Even more wine than dancing in fact. And . . . and . . . a lot of cheese?

Urgh!

She shot out of the bed, tripping over the blanket as it caught around her legs, then hot-footed it to the en suite toilet.

Ten minutes later, Lucy felt simultaneously completely disgusting and a whole lot better. She scooped up handfuls of cold water at the sink and washed her face, then cleaned her teeth with her finger and paste from a half-used tube that Caro must have left behind when she moved out.

Lucy slunk back to the bedroom, cracked out a couple of pills and downed them along with the entire pint of water. Then she sank back down onto the bed with a groan.

Give it ten minutes and she was bound to be fine, wasn't she? It was only a hangover. Sure, she hadn't had a hangover like this in more than a decade, but it had been worth it. Actually - that was a total guess considering the gaping holes in what she could remember from the night before.

As she snuggled back down into the blankets, she

tried to piece the bits together. She had absolutely no memory of how the evening had ended, nor how she'd landed up back here rather than at her own place. The bits she could remember were pretty spectacular though, and as she grinned into the cosy darkness under her covers, snapshots started to replay themselves. The limo ride there. Arriving at the vineyard and being ushered into a private room. Then the girls sat around, drank bubbly and nibbled on tiny taste explosions that were delivered by smiling waiters while she was treated to professional hair and makeup, followed by an outfit she'd long-coveted from Caro's shop that Sue had arranged as a gift for her.

'Hello?!'

Lucy flinched. She might be feeling a tiny bit better, but she really wasn't up for seeing anyone yet.

'Luce?'

There was a knock at the bedroom door, and Lucy grunted in response, not even sticking her head out from under the covers.

'Oh good, you drank the water!'

Caro's voice was muffled by the blanket over Lucy's head, but even from inside her cocoon, Caro sounded annoyingly bright.

Heaving a sigh, Lucy popped her head back out into the over-bright room.

'Morning, bright eyes!' laughed Caro.

'Urgh!' said Lucy, blinking at her. 'Why are you so okay?'

'One of the up-sides of being preggers,' laughed Caro, 'I didn't drink a vineyard dry last night - so I don't have the hangover to show for it!'

'Alright for some,' muttered Lucy.

Caro just let out a chuckle, grabbed the empty pint-glass from Lucy's bedside table and went to refill it.

Lucy struggled up in the bed and did her best to make sure she looked at least half-way human by the time her friend came back in.

'Drink!' said Caro.

'You're bossy!' muttered Lucy.

'Mum in training,' laughed Caro, handing her the glass and then easing herself down onto the double bed.

The next thing Lucy knew, Caro had swung her legs up and settled down onto the pillows next to her.

'Be my guest!' laughed Lucy, then winced as her head rumbled in anger.

'I might not be hungover, but *am* completely wiped out,' sighed Caro. 'I'm too old and too up the duff to be doing that kinda thing too often!'

Lucy nodded. 'Know what you mean. Not about the baby thing - but I swear hangovers weren't this bad a few years ago.'

'You'll be okay,' said Caro, giving her a gentle nudge. Get that water in you and wait for the pills to kick in and you'll be ready for some breakfast.'

'Not the B-word, I beg you!' groaned Lucy.

'Okay . . . but I brought everything you need for a fry-up!' said Caro, with an evil grin.

Lucy grabbed one of the cushions from the pile next to her and bopped Caro in the face, making her laugh.

'How come we're here?' asked Lucy after they'd sat in silence for a few minutes, while Lucy had concentrated on the image of icebergs to try to combat the renewed surging sensations the mention of a fry-up had caused.

'Well,' said Caro, 'you weren't in a fit state to walk to your place. We pulled up outside to let Scarlet out because her mum was meeting us here, and you piled out after her - yelling about an after-party in the pub!'

'Oh god, I did, didn't I?!' groaned Lucy as the memory snuck back in.

Caro was giggling now. 'The poor old taxi driver wasn't very keen about letting you back in once you'd got out, so I paid him to drop Amber and Violet up to Bamton Hall. Violet was three sheets to the wind too, so I thought it was best to dispatch her for a sleepover with Horace and Amber! Emmy and Eve helped me get you upstairs, though frankly, it would have been easier without them!'

'I'm soooo sorry,' said Lucy, covering her face with her hands.

'No big deal,' laughed Caro. 'As soon as you got in bed, you stopped trying to force us to go downstairs for a "nightcrap," Caro was now giggling so hard she had to stop to catch her breath.

'*Nightcrap*?!' demanded Lucy.

'I think you meant nightcap? It was so funny. Emmy kept repeating everything you said, and Eve was doing that thing where she was trying to sound super sensible and sober.'

'Ah yes, only the truly plastered try that one!' Lucy grinned weakly.

'Well, she rather negated it when she started singing *It's Raining Men* at the top of her voice on the way back downstairs,' said Caro.

'Did those two get home okay?' asked Lucy.

'Yeah - Jon came over and walked them both back over to Dragonfly cottage. Eve crashed out over there for the night, and after I got you sorted, Sam took me home.'

'Sam? He came all the way down. Oh god!' chuckled Lucy, 'I've got some serious apologising to do, haven't I?!'

'Hardly,' laughed Lucy. 'Sam was already here - he'd waited downstairs for us to come back. Anyway, if anyone's going to have to apologise to the whole village, it'll be Emmy and Eve!'

'Why?' asked Lucy.

'Well, Jon texted me when they got back. I think there was quite a loud rendition of Robbie Williams's *Angels* as they walked through the middle of the village, and then Emmy puked over someone's front garden wall.'

Lucy laughed so hard at that she thought she was going to follow suit for a second. 'That's going to end up in the village newsletter, isn't it?!' she spluttered.

Caro nodded. 'Yup! Or at least, it will if I have anything to do with it!'

'I hope Scarlet's okay,' sighed Lucy, 'I feel like we've corrupted her!'

'Hardly,' said Caro. 'She only had a couple of glasses of bubbly and was the most together out of the lot of you. She danced like a lunatic but bless her she still offered to stay and help me get you into bed!'

'Sounds like I need to give her a Christmas bonus!' said Lucy.

'You mean a bribe to forget what a lightweight her boss is?' said Caro.

'Yeah . . . that too!' said Lucy with a huge sigh. For some reason, talking about Scarlet had just managed to shift her sore head right back into work mode. The brief respite from worrying about her Christmas and wedding to-do lists was suddenly over. A wave of prickly panic washed over her - she didn't have time to slob around in bed!

'Where are you going?' asked Caro in surprise as Lucy sat up and swung her legs off the bed with purpose.

'I've got so much to do!' said Lucy, doing her best to ignore the ominous rolling from her stomach as she searched the room for some clothes. All she could find was the crumpled vintage dress she'd changed into for the party the night before.

'Calm down,' sighed Caro, shuffling to the edge of the bed herself, hoiking herself to her feet and wandering over to the wooden chair that sat underneath the window. 'Here - your clothes from before you changed last night,' she said, snagging a stuffed canvas tote from the back of the chair and tossing it to Lucy. 'Sue put some fresh undies in for you too!' she smiled.

'And that's why she's a keeper,' said Lucy.

As soon as she was dressed, Lucy's panic about how much she had to get done was threatening to overwhelm her and she was itching to get downstairs.

'Seriously - you *really* need to calm down!' said Caro.

'But I've got to get the decorations up in the pub!' said Lucy with a hint of panic in her voice. 'I've *got* to - before we open up for the day - otherwise, I'm going to run out of time and-'

'Breathe, woman!' said Caro, shaking her head.

'At least I'm already here, I guess,' said Lucy, bustling around and ignoring Caro's attempts to get her to slow down. 'I'd better call Sue and see if she can bring the decs down for me and . . .'

'Let's just go downstairs and see what's what first, shall we?' said Caro.

'Okay,' said Lucy, deflating a bit, her head thudding in time with the nervy pound of her heart.

'Leave your stuff up here for now,' Caro added, nodding at the crumpled dress.

Lucy nodded and bustled towards the door, heading out onto the stone steps that lead down the back of the pub.

The moment the fresh air hit her, Lucy felt a little bit better. She paused at the top of the staircase and sucked a lungful of crisp air in, while screwing her eyes up at just how bright it was out here. The sky was a merciless blue, and there had clearly been quite a hard frost. The sun had already burned most of it off the field behind the pub, leaving a fringe of crispy white around the edges under the hedges where its rays hadn't yet been able to reach.

'Shit - what time is it?' she asked. She'd assumed it was first-thing but . . .

'Just coming up to eleven,' said Caro from behind her.

'Noooo!' squeaked Lucy, jogging down the stone steps.

She needed to get on with things. The pub should be open in mere minutes. Damn, she'd have to put up the Christmas decorations around the customers. That was never a good idea and-

'Hold up!' said Caro, taking the steps more

cautiously. 'You forget I'm *with child!'* she laughed, holding her hands over her bump for dramatic effect when she reached the bottom.

Lucy paused and turned back to Caro, a wash of guilt flooding through her . . . or maybe that was just her hangover - it was kind of difficult to tell by this point. Whatever it was, she felt awful.

'I'm so sorry,' she said, holding her arm out for Caro to take. 'I told you - I'm turning into an awful cross between Bridezilla and some kind of Christmas cracker!'

'No, you're not!' said Caro firmly, taking her arm and pulling her to a complete standstill for a moment. 'But you are zooming around so fast, you're in danger of missing out on things!'

'But that's what I'm worried about - I don't want to miss things - I *keep* forgetting stuff!' said Lucy, fighting down a weird swell of tears. 'I wouldn't even have a wedding dress if it wasn't for you!'

'I didn't say *missing things,'* said Caro gently. 'I said missing *out* on things.'

'What's the difference?' asked Lucy.

Instead of answering, Caro let go of Lucy's arm, gripped her shoulders and firmly turned her so that she was facing the back of the pub. Then she pointed up at the roof.

'What on earth . . .?!' gasped Lucy, staring wide-eyed at the pair of Santa legs sticking out of the chimney pot.

'Looks like the elves have been busy!' said Caro with a grin.

'I *love* it!' said Lucy, a sudden smile spreading across her face.

'Well you've got Sue and Sam to thank for that particular spectacle, I think!' laughed Caro.

'I'd better get in there and start on the inside!' said Lucy, taking a couple of steps forwards.

Caro pulled her to a halt again. 'I know I'm ruining the surprise, but it's all done. Everyone came down last night and missioned it while we were out!'

Lucy's mouth dropped open. 'You're kidding me?'

'Nope, you're all sorted. Sounds like they had a blast, too. Sam's in there now, opening up for you, and Scarlet's already in to help him out - so there really isn't any rush, okay?'

Lucy sagged a bit and stared up at the Santa legs again. 'I don't deserve you lot,' she sighed.

'Rubbish. We all adore you. And Sue. And we just want you to have the most amazing wedding and Christmas, okay?!'

Lucy stared at Caro for a moment and then nodded, unable to stop her lip from quivering.

'Before we go in,' said Caro, a slight frown creasing her forehead, 'last night, before things started getting a bit messy, you said something . . .' Caro paused a moment, and then, clearly steeling herself, carried on. 'You said something about Sue not being sure about the wedding?'

Lucy screwed her nose up for a moment. Shit. That must have slipped out after a drink or two. Otherwise, there was no way she'd have let that deepest of deep fears out into the world. She didn't even want to say it out loud again now. She really, *really* didn't want to . . . but Caro was watching her intently, waiting for her answer.

'I think she's struggling because her parents never knew. About me, I mean.'

'That's hard,' said Caro.

'It is. And . . . well, there's nothing I can do to help her with it. They're gone.' Lucy shrugged. 'But sometimes, if Sue mentions it when her guard is down, it's like she's dreading getting married without them there, without their approval - or their . . . their consent, I guess?' she let out a long sigh. 'I just don't want her to regret getting married to me. I don't want her to get cold feet either. It's like, at times, it puts some kind of a wall up between us - just for a second.'

Lucy swallowed hard. Talking about this wasn't helping. If anything, it was making it feel more like a real problem than something she'd just built up in her head.

'Sue loves you, Luce,' said Caro quietly. 'Heart and soul. It's so obvious - and I don't think *anything* in the world could stop her marrying you on the twenty-third.'

Lucy nodded, biting her lip to stop the ridiculous quivering she didn't seem to be able to control. She knew that Sue loved her. Really, she did - but there was still something unspoken between the pair of them that felt like it needed to be resolved.

'Come on,' sighed Lucy, deciding to change the subject before she became a blubbering mess. 'I think I might be almost ready to face that fry-up!'

CHAPTER 6

SUE

'*P*ull!'

Sue followed the clay disc across the sky with her gun and squeezed the trigger. She couldn't help the grin that spread across her face as she watched it explode into fragments.

'Oi oi,' boomed Horace, 'looks like we've got a ringer here!'

Sue broke the gun and turned to the others, giving them a little bow. The guys were cheering, but Amber, Emmy and Eve were jumping up and down, clapping and squealing.

'Nice shooting!' said Sam, coming over and taking the gun from her. 'Five out of five? Why do I get the feeling there's something about your past that you're not telling us?' he smirked.

'What, like she's actually a trained super sniper?' laughed Horace.

'Or a spy?!' said Sam.

Sue rolled her eyes at the pair of them. 'Hardly! I've just done this before, that's all.'

'Ah, so you *are* a ringer?'

'Maybe!' grinned Sue. 'Anyway, I'll get out of the way - it's Sam's turn!'

'Oh yeah,' he groaned, rolling his eyes, 'I drew the short straw having to follow a performance like that!'

Sue gave him a quick pat on the arm and beat a hasty retreat to join the others in the designated "safe zone".

'Great job!' said Mark, smiling at her.

Sue grinned back. Her old friend looked so insanely different in his checked flat cap and Barbour jacket compared to his usual Sunday vicar getup. She guessed that he was probably handsome if that was your kind of thing.

'Yeah,' said Amber, sidling up to her and digging her in the ribs with her elbow. 'If I'd known you were some kind of Olympic-level shooting champion on the sly, I might have set up something a little bit more challenging!'

'This is perfect,' said Sue, looking around at her friends all gathered together - each of them wearing the required costume of a flat cap or ridiculous deer-stalker, along with cord trousers, waistcoats and Barbour jackets. The dress code had been *country gentleman*, and everyone looked fantastic - though, it had to be said that Horace looked no different to how he normally dressed. 'The only thing that would make today any better would be -'

'A stripper?' asked Emmy, giving Sue a naughty wink.

'Nope,' she said, rolling her eyes. 'I was just going to say - if Lucy and Caro were here.'

'Well, you two were the ones who decided not to invite each other to your hen dos!' said Mark with a laugh.

'Yeah, and the hilarious thing is that you've both whined about it in exactly the same way,' said Eve.

'Aw!' said Sue. 'Did Luce really want me there?'

'Are you mad? She missed you like crazy!' said Emmy.

'I know the feeling,' sighed Sue.

'Urgh, get me a bucket!' giggled Amber. 'Anyway, as for Caro - I *do* get why she decided that loud bangs, live ammo and a pregnant belly weren't her idea of a match made in heaven.'

'Oh, me too!' said Sue, nodding. 'Besides, the pair of them are keeping each other company and doing the last-minute alterations to Luce's dress, I think!'

'Is she all better from the other night then?' asked Eve, wincing slightly.

'Only just,' grinned Sue. 'I'm not sure I've ever seen her so hungover. You guys definitely did a good job there!'

'It wasn't just Lucy, trust me,' said Eve, rubbing her

head as if the memory of her own hangover still haunted her.

'So I've heard,' said Sue, raising an amused eyebrow. 'Horace said Violet didn't emerge from his spare room until after midday - and that's after he'd delivered two cups of tea and plenty of rich tea biscuits, apparently.'

'Aw - I love that he's so sweet to her,' said Emmy, watching the pair of them as they cheered one of Sam's shots.

'He really is,' said Amber with a smile, 'though she'd hate to think anyone noticed.'

'I think it's wonderful,' said Mark. 'Take it from me, that'll be the next wedding we celebrate here in Little Bamton!'

'Do you know something we don't?' said Amber, raising her eyebrows.

Mark shook his head. 'Just a vicar's intuition,' he said with a grin.

'And that's why I love that you're Sue's best man,' said Eve. 'You're a total closet romantic!'

'Yeah,' said Amber, 'though I'd have thought you'd be running the entire show at the wedding rather than just being best man,' said Amber.

Emmy batted her across the back of the head, knocking her flat cap flying.

'Oi!' she protested. 'What? I'm just saying . . .'

'You're about as subtle as a brick, my dear,' said Will, who'd just joined their little gaggle. He scooped her hat off the grass, gave it a shake and settled it back onto her head, kissing her nose in the process.

'There were a number of reasons,' said Mark easily, clearly not taking any offence. 'They didn't want a church wedding, they wanted to support Bamton Hall-'

'Exactly!' said Sue, cutting in. 'The place means a lot to us - we spent a ridiculous amount of time canoodling in those gardens when we first got together.'

Will let out a loud wolf-whistle, making them all jump.

'Plus,' said Sue, taking Mark's arm and grinning at him, 'I wanted Mark all to myself for the day - not in work mode, but in best-friend mode.'

'So . . . let me get this straight,' said Will, 'you've got Mark and Amber as your, erm . . . best people?'

Sue nodded.

'And me, Caro and Eve are Lucy's bridesmaids,' beamed Emmy.

'Lucy's mum's giving her away,' said Eve with a gentle smile.

'What about you, Sue?' asked Amber. 'Who's giving you away?'

'Goodness, you *are* on a roll,' muttered Emmy, rolling her eyes.

'Well,' said Sue, 'no one really. My parents aren't around anymore, so . . .' she trailed off and shrugged. Damn it, she thought she'd been doing so well, putting that to the back of her mind, but every time it popped up like this out of the blue, it was like someone was stabbing her in the heart.

It was ridiculous really - she'd done her grieving for both her parents years ago. But there was something about this whole wedding lark that made things feel fresh - the wound felt raw again.

'I'm really sorry,' said Amber, grabbing Sue's hand and giving it a squeeze. 'I didn't mean to upset you!'

'It's okay. It's just . . . well . . . I really miss them. Marrying Luce is the most important thing in the world to me - and it . . . it just really hurts that they're not going to be there to share it with us. I never even got to introduce them to Lucy.'

Sue stopped talking abruptly. This was ridiculous. This was her hen-do, her big send-off, and all she wanted to do right now was cry.

'They would have loved nothing more than seeing you so happy and content,' said Mark gently.

Sue took a deep breath and nodded awkwardly.

'Hey guys, why all the long faces?' said Sam, bounding over towards them. 'This *is* meant to be a party, right?!'

Sue nodded. 'Right.' She forced a wide smile on her face and decided to do her very best not to depress the crap out of everyone.

'I just put my foot in it . . . as usual,' sighed Amber.

'Nah, it's fine,' said Sue, giving her a playful nudge. 'I was just having a moment of missing my folks, that's all,' she said to Sam.

'Well, when we're done here, I think there are drinks in the offing?' said Sam, raising his eyebrows at Mark, who nodded. 'Cool. Then we'll all toast your parents.'

'Sounds good,' said Sue, nodding. 'Right - let's go and watch how young Davy gets on, shall we?' she said. She moved forwards to get a better view as Eve's son lifted his gun for his first shot and crossed her fingers that the others would follow suit and let her drop the subject of her parents before she became a blubbering mess. 'Go on, Davy boy!' she yelled.

'Hey!' said Sam, weaving his way between the rustic, barrel-top tables in the "shooting lodge", which was actually just a jazzed-up barn with plenty of alcohol on tap.

'Hey Sam,' said Sue.

'Do ya fancy a quick wander outside with me?' he slurred ever so slightly. 'I need some fresh air!'

''Scuse me,' said Sue, smiling at Eve and Finn.

'It's fine, looks like Sam's need is most definitely greater than ours!' laughed Finn.

Sue got steadily to her feet. Most of her friends were thoroughly merry by this point, but not her. She'd had a couple of pints and then decided to switch to soft drinks. She was feeling emotional enough as it was -

she didn't need to become an out-of-control, blub-bering mess if she could help it.

She followed Sam out into the chilly December air. It was already dark and the stars peeped out here and there between the clouds that floated like heavy galleons across the winter night sky.

Sue took a deep breath and let the air cool her warm cheeks. It was really rather lovely out here. The lodge was surrounded by large, flaming outdoor candles that trailed away and illuminated a walkway around the little paddock it stood in.

'Shall we?' she asked, raising her eyebrows at Sam, nodding to the circular walk.

'Good call!' said Sam, who'd been staring quietly up at the sky, completely lost in his own thoughts for a moment.

'You okay?' asked Sue, thrusting her hands into her cord trouser pockets as they began to amble between the flickering patches of torchlight. 'I know this is a difficult time of year for you.'

Sam nodded, not saying anything for a moment, and Sue bit her lip, forcing herself to stay quiet and leave the space open for him to talk if he wanted to.

'It is,' he said quietly. 'In one way, it feels like I lost Amy just yesterday. But then, with Caro arriving last Christmas, and all the incredible things that have happened this year . . . I don't know . . . it also feels like light-years ago and that maybe this time of year can be joyful again.'

Sam stopped talking abruptly and let out a huge sigh, causing Sue to reach out and grab his arm.

'I love Caro,' he said. 'I didn't think I'd ever get to love anyone like this again. And I'm so excited to start a family together. But . . . I still love Amy too. I think I always will.'

'Of course you will,' said Sue, shrugging. 'Love like that doesn't just evaporate.'

'But there are times I feel so guilty,' sighed Sam. 'I mean, that I'm in love with Caro and still in love with Amy and . . . me and Caro get this shot at an amazing life together.'

'Sam - Amy would be thrilled. You know she would. You were the most important thing in her whole world. Even more important than Christmas, and that's saying something. For what it's worth, I think she'd have loved Caro.'

Sam nodded. 'I know she would. And me and Caro have talked about her loads. That's never been weird. Caro's even said that she wants the baby to grow up knowing Amy's name and as much about her as we can share to make sure her memory's always fresh. I just don't know how I got so lucky!'

Sue squeezed his arm. 'Because you're an amazing person, Sam. You deserve every single bit of happiness that comes your way. Don't you ever forget that, okay?'

'Thanks, mate,' said Sam, his voice coming out low and gruff. He patted her on the back before clearing his throat. 'Erm, your turn. Do you mind if I ask you something . . . a bit awkward?'

Sue raised her eyebrows and glanced at Sam, his handsome face was lit by the dancing torchlight and he looked serious.

'Sure,' she said, though a strange feeling of apprehension ran through her.

'Have you had any second thoughts about marrying Lucy?'

'What!?' gasped Sue. 'No! Why would you even ask that?'

'Well . . . I'm not really sure I should be telling you this, but I think someone has to give you the heads up. Caro mentioned that Lucy had a bit of a wobble on her hen do, and then again yesterday morning when she was mega-hungover.'

'A wobble? You mean *she's* having second thoughts about the wedding?' said Sue. She felt like her knees had just been taken over by a pair of drunk jellyfish, and little darts of white-hot panic shot through her.

'No!' said Sam. 'Sorry, I didn't mean that. Caro seemed to think that Lucy's worried about *you* having second thoughts.'

'But why?' gasped Sue.

'I think it had something to do with your parents,' he said, pausing on the path and turning to face her.

'Oh . . . shit,' said Sue. 'I mean . . . shit,' she said again, desperately trying to get her thoughts in order. Sam was staring at her with so much worry on his face that part of her wanted to laugh at just how quickly the jungle drums could start beating in a small village if you weren't careful. Not that Sam would say anything to anyone, but if Lucy'd mentioned this while she'd been plastered on her hen do, then maybe Violet had heard something. If she *had*, that would mean that everyone in the South West would have the wrong end of the stick by this point.

'Sue?' prompted Sam.

'Sorry,' she sighed. 'Look, there's nothing I've been more certain of in my entire life than the fact that I want to spend the rest of it married to Lucy.'

Sam nodded, a smile returning to his face. 'But?'

'But I miss my parents,' she said simply. 'And a massive event like this has just made me feel it more keenly. I'll never be able to introduce Lucy. They'll never get to see us tie the knot. I mean - I know all that, I'm dealing with it. But I just want them to be part of the whole thing – even in a tiny way and . . . and . . .'

'Hey!' said Sam gently as a couple of tears slid down her face and plopped off her chin.

'Sorry,' she sniffed, wiping her eyes with the back of her hands. She didn't cry. This wasn't her. She needed to pull herself together. 'Look, I've been driving myself mad because I lost my mum's wedding ring up at the allotment. I used to wear it on a cord around my neck after she passed - and then one day, when I was digging up there, it was just gone.' She took a deep, shuddering breath. 'I know it's ridiculous, and that it's just a little band of metal . . . but it feels like my last link to them, and I can't imagine getting married to Lucy without being able to put that ring on her finger!'

'Have you ever tried to find it?' asked Sam, setting off again so that they slowly started to head back towards the barn where the hen-do was in full swing.

Sue nodded. 'I borrowed my nephew's metal detector but never had any luck. And it's been years - though I always keep my eyes peeled when I'm up there.' She shrugged. 'I guess there's not much chance I'll ever see it again. I need to get over it and buy Lucy a ring she'll love. That's what's really important. I've picked one out . . . but I still haven't actually bought it yet. I just keep hoping for some kind of miracle.'

'Well,' said Sam, 'how about we have one last look at the allotments?'

'I don't know, Sam,' sighed Sue.

'If it's this important to you, it's got to be worth it, hasn't it? Nothing ventured, after all!'

'What were you thinking?' she asked.

'Well, my dad and Caro's dad are both members of a local metal detecting club. I bet you anything they'd all love an excuse to check out the allotments! You never know what else they might find - and there's a chance they might rediscover your mum's ring while they're at it!'

'Do you really think they'd be willing to do that for me?'

'Are you kidding?' laughed Sam. 'That lot will jump

at the chance to check over a virgin patch of ground! I'll call my dad first thing in the morning. Then, if they don't have any luck, you can buy Luce that ring.'

'Okay,' said Sue, 'you're on. Thank you so much!'

'It's on one condition,' he said seriously.

'Oh yes?'

'Yeah. Make sure you talk to Lucy? She needs to know exactly how you feel.'

'You've got it,' said Sue, patting him gratefully on the arm.

CHAPTER 7

'*N*ot long to go now, Luce!' said Emmy, looking for a space in between all the holly cuttings on the table to plonk a cup of tea down for her friend. 'Nervous?'

Lucy smiled and shook her head, even as the nerves swooped through her stomach. 'Not even slightly,' she lied fluently. 'I do wish I was a bit more . . . ready, though?'

'But everything's good to go, isn't it?' said Emmy, sitting back down opposite her, placing her own cup carefully down and pulling her protective gloves back on.

Lucy shrugged, picked up a sprig of holly and carefully wired it onto the wreath she was working on. This morning was turning out to be a blissful distraction from fretting about all things wedding. She'd promised to help Emmy out with making wreaths to sell on Grandad Jim's Flower Cart in the lead up to Christmas day in exchange for Emmy doing her wedding flowers for her. It didn't exactly feel like a fair exchange to Lucy who really wanted to pay her friend, but Emmy wasn't having any of it.

'Well,' said Emmy, 'let's think. You've got your dress sorted and Caro's done the alterations. Amber's done her bit up at the hall - and the flowers are going to look amazing, so you don't need to worry about that. Oh . . . don't tell me you forgot to send invites out?!' she said, raising her eyebrows.

'No - that's done,' laughed Lucy. 'Mostly because it was Sue's job, not mine!'

'So you're ready!' said Emmy. 'What's there left to worry about?'

'I'm not sure,' sighed Lucy. 'I feel like I've been working through my damn to-do lists for so long that I'm convinced there's something I've missed.'

'Time to relax, my sweet,' said Emmy, clipping a stem and adding it to her wreath before reaching for some deep red, silk ribbon.

'I know - you're right. I've just got to nip into town and collect Sue's wedding ring later when I pick up mum and your Aunty Ali from the train station . . . and I think that's me done for the day!'

'I can't wait to see Aunty Ali,' said Emmy with a happy sigh. 'I can't believe I've been living here since the spring, and she's not even been back once.'

'Clearly the life of a nomad suits her!' said Lucy.

'How do you feel about having her back at Dragonfly Cottage? Are you worried that once she's back she's not going to want to leave again?'

Emmy shrugged her shoulders. 'Not really. I mean, I love living here with Jon - it's the most wonderful thing in the world for us that it's just been so effortless to try out living together. It just happened kind of . . .' she trailed away, searching for the right word.

'Organically?' asked Lucy, waving a frond of dried grass at her friend.

'Exactly!' said Emmy. 'Just nice and natural, no pressure. But if Ali did want to move back, I think Jon and I know by this point that we'd want to look for a home together. And I know Ali would support us all the way.'

'Do you think you'd leave Little Bamton?' asked Lucy, trying to keep her tone light, but feeling secretly horrified at the idea of lovely Emmy and her flower stall disappearing from village life. Emmy might have only been around since the spring, but it felt like she'd always been part of life here somehow.

'Not on your nelly!' laughed Emmy. 'This is it for me. Home. And I know that Jon feels the same way. I mean, I've got the flower field here, and we *have* vaguely talked about looking into getting planning for a little eco-cabin, or one of those cute *tiny-homes* so that I could be with my flowers all the time. We could rent somewhere in the meantime, though that's always a bit of a challenge around here!'

'Well actually,' said Lucy, 'my cottage will be up for grabs as a rental sometime in the spring if you do need to look for somewhere to tide you over.'

'Really?!' said Emmy. 'I love your place. Are you really leaving it?'

Lucy nodded. It was one of the things she and Sue had discussed over and over again. They both owned their own cottages in the village, but Sue's had a huge garden, not dissimilar to the one at Dragonfly Cottage. It had a lovely old apple tree, lots of space for all Sue's veggie experiments and plenty of bright and beautiful flower beds. It was like an outdoor extension to the cottage itself, and Sue spent a great deal of her time out there - using it a bit like an outdoor living room.

Lucy's cottage was incredibly cute but absolutely minuscule, with just a tiny postage-stamp of a front garden. Lucy loved it and it had suited her down to the ground as a busy singleton with a pub to run, but this year she'd spent most of her time between Sue's place and the pub - so much so that Sue's cottage already felt like home.

'Wow,' said Emmy, smiling at her, 'look at all of us, so grown-up!'

Lucy spluttered out a laugh. 'I don't think we get to say things like that so soon after my hen-do, do you?'

Emmy pulled a face. 'Huh, you might have a point there. I don't think I'm going to live that down any time soon. Do you reckon you could maybe avoid telling Aunty Ali about my little puking incident?'

'Only if you keep schtum around my mum about having to pour me into bed above the pub because that's as far as I could stagger!' replied Lucy, giving Emmy a wink.

'I'll high-five to that,' said Emmy, slapping her gloved hand against Lucy's. 'And . . . do you reckon, when you're ready to rent out your place . . . could you maybe give me and Jon a quick nudge before going public with it? Just in case there are any developments with Ali wanting to come home? I promise we'd be model tenants!'

'You're on,' said Lucy. 'You guys get first dibs!'

'Mum!' squealed Lucy, jogging along the train platform and throwing her arms around her mother. What was it about seeing her mum that made her revert straight back to a six-year-old?

'Hello, my love,' said her mum, her voice muffled by layers of scarf and hair as Lucy hugged her tight. 'It's so wonderful to see you!'

'You too!' said Lucy, pulling back slightly and grabbing her mum's hands to stare at her and drink her in. 'Where's your case?' she asked suddenly, realising that her mum only had her handbag slung over her shoulder.

'Ali's got it!' she grinned.

'You know Ali?' said Lucy, distracted.

'Of course! I met her . . . oh, erm . . . about four Christmases ago when I came down to stay? You remember? We've kept in contact ever since. Such a fascinating trip she's been on - she told me all about her travels. Made the journey fly by!'

'Certainly did!' came a voice from behind Lucy.

She whirled around only to come face to face with someone who was only partly recognisable as Emmy's Aunty, and her old friend.

'Look at you, Ali!' squealed Lucy, grabbing hold of Ali's hands and staring at her. 'You look gorgeous!'

Lucy couldn't take her eyes off her. She'd had her hair cropped super-short, and it was now a beautiful, salty-grey, curly crop that made Ali's hazel eyes stand out a mile in her freckled and tanned face. She might have joked earlier with Emmy about Ali's nomad life-style suiting her, but here was physical proof of just how true that was. The woman looked about a decade younger than last time she'd set eyes on her.

'Quit it, you!' laughed Ali as Lucy continued to eyeball her.

'I just haven't seen you for so long!' said Lucy.

'I know!' said Ali. 'And look what you've gone and done in that time missus - found out that the love of your life was right there all along . . . and now you're getting married! See, I seem to remember during my goodbye drinks that you were busy telling me you'd given up looking and had firm plans to become a mad cat lady and dying an old maid?'

Lucy's mum snorted with laughter. 'I think Lucy was born a mad cat lady, you know.'

'Gee, thanks mum,' sniggered Lucy, rolling her eyes.

'I'm just saying! When all the other little girls were begging for whatever ridiculous pink plastic thing that was new and trendy, you were busy begging me for an old-fashioned hand-knit instead!'

'That's because no one knits quite like you, mum!' said Lucy, linking arms with her, and taking the handle of her suitcase from Ali's grip so that she could manage her own canvas bag more easily.

'Flattery will get you everywhere, but that's hardly the point, love,' laughed her mum. 'What I'm trying to say is that you've always done things your own way. And I've always been very proud of that.'

'Oh hell,' laughed Lucy, 'let's get back to the car before I start blubbing right here on the platform!'

She lead the pair of them to where she'd left her car and they loaded the boot with their bags.

'Erm - are either of you desperate to head straight back to Little Bamton?' asked Lucy, hesitantly. 'I know you've both had a long trip, but there's one thing I need to do in town. I can always pop you both back home and then drive back in, though. I had hoped to get here in time to get it done before your train arrived, but I ended up losing track of time while I was helping Emmy with her wreaths!'

'I'm not in any kind of rush,' said Ali with a shrug. 'What about you, Rose?'

Lucy's mum shook her head. 'Lead the way, dear!' she said, hoisting her handbag securely onto her shoulder. 'I could do with stretching my legs after all that sitting down anyway. Then we'll enjoy a nice cake and a cuppa when we get back. What's the mission?'

'Well,' said Lucy, 'I need to collect Sue's wedding ring from the jeweller's in town.'

'You've left it until *two days* before the wedding?' gasped her mother, incredulously.

Lucy nodded. She couldn't help but crack a smile. It was the exact tone her mum had always used on her when she'd left her homework until the last minute.

'You think that's bad,' she said with a wicked grin, 'I only chose my wedding dress last week!'

'What?' laughed Ali. 'Goodness, you do like living on the edge!'

'That's rich, coming from you,' said Rose, 'after what you were telling me about skydiving in Scotland.'

'Skydiving?' said Lucy, pausing to stare at Ali.

'Don't look at me like that!' laughed Ali. 'I may be old, but I'm definitely not past it!'

'I wouldn't dream of saying you were either of those things,' said Lucy seriously. 'But . . . skydiving?'

Ali shrugged. 'I've had lots of adventures this year. Including skydiving. Nothing wrong with throwing yourself out of a perfectly good plane now and then!'

'Nothing right about it either, though,' chortled Rose.

'Come on,' said Lucy, ushering them towards the

little jewellery shop on the high street, 'let's pick up this ring and then I think we need to find a decent cuppa and a piece of cake. I want to hear all about your adventures, but I feel like I might need a sugar-hit to survive the tale!'

'Gerald!' said Sue with a huge grin as she hurried over to greet Caro's father. 'Thank you so much for convincing the guys to do this for me!'

'Are you kidding?' laughed Gerald, holding out one hand to shake Sue's while keeping a firm grip on an absolute monster of a machine with his other hand. 'Give us a new patch of ground to play on and we're like a bunch of big kids! It can be an absolute nightmare to get permission sometimes, so this is a treat.'

'Well, you're doing me a huge favour - so thank you!' said Sue sincerely.

About half a dozen men were gathering around them now, all lugging some serious kit, headphones dangling around their necks and trowels tucked into their tool belts. Clearly, these guys meant business.

'Sue? I'm Harry, Sam's dad,' said a tall man who was

the spitting image of her friend - though perhaps a little bit more crumpled around the edges. 'I think we've met before, but several years ago.'

Sue nodded, smiling at him. She didn't want to be the one to point out that they'd met at Amy's funeral. 'It's lovely to see you again!' she said instead. 'Thank you for helping me out!'

'It's my pleasure. Sam thinks very highly of you and your bride-to-be. I know how much you've done for him . . . it's nice to be able to at least *try* to do something for you in return.'

'So,' said one of the other guys, his eyes roving keenly across the expanse of scruffy vegetable beds - now mostly bare apart from the patch of sprouts, a few other late winter veggies and some stumpy bits and pieces that hadn't quite been cleared away yet. 'What does this ring we're hunting for actually look like?'

'Oh,' said Sue, 'it's a simple wedding band - quite a wide one - and it's got a single, small ruby set into it. Or at least, it did when I lost it . . . I wouldn't be surprised if that's long gone by now though,' she sighed sadly.

'Maybe not,' said Harry, giving her a reassuring pat on the shoulder. 'A lot of treasures turn up in perfect condition - even when they've been buried for centuries. Your ring might have been sitting there, exactly where you dropped it - just waiting to make its way back to you.'

'I really hope so,' said Sue, strangely comforted by

this slightly poetic stance on things. It had felt a bit like having her heart cut out with a blunt spoon when she'd realised what had happened.

'Well, we'll give it a go!' said Gerald. Sue noticed his fingers twitching against his metal detector. He was clearly very keen to get started despite the thick drizzle that was now falling in an icy mist around them, clinging to everyone's hair and leaving tiny, glittering droplets in the bushiest of eyebrows.

'Is there anything we need to avoid trampling?' asked one of the guys Sue didn't know.

'Not much,' she shrugged. 'Alf's picked most of the sprouts now - but if you could avoid the small patch that's still standing I'd appreciate it. And I'm overwintering carrots just over here in this patch with the white string around it - so if you could leave them in one piece so that we can enjoy them with our Christmas lunch, that'd be much appreciated. Oh, and there are still some potatoes in over there, though they won't mind in the slightest if you tread between the rows!' she said.

'Perfect!' said Harry. 'And . . . any idea where you lost it? I know it could so easily have shifted, but . . .'

Sue shook her head sadly. 'I had it on a cord around my neck. I know it was still there when I got here because it was a hot day and I yanked off my jumper and nearly garrotted myself with the thing in the process. I bet that's what loosened the knot, actually. But then, when I was gathering my things to leave, I

bent down to collect some plant labels I'd finished with
and the cord just dropped onto the ground in front of
me - the ring was long gone.

'I looked everywhere - but I'd been hoeing up potatoes and digging things over, and I'd even turned a
compost heap that day so . . . it could be anywhere up
here. It *could* be just lying on the top somewhere . . . or
buried pretty deep by now.'

'Alright Sue,' said Gerald, 'we'll do our best for you.
Of course, anything else we find we'll hand over so you
can check it out with the others who work up here too
- you never know what might turn up!'

'Thanks, guys! I'm going to nip down to the pub to
give Lucy a hand settling her mum in, but I'll be back in
about an hour with a round of hot drinks and toasties,
okay?'

There was a rousing chorus of cheers at this news
and Sue gave them all one last grateful wave and then
beat a hasty retreat. She wanted to leave them to get on
with it. She could tell they were excited to divvy up the
site between them, and when she turned back for a last
look before heading back through the five-barred gate
towards the village square, they were all huddled
together and there was much excited pointing and
twiddling of knobs going on. Today wasn't the day for
it, but she'd quite like to have a go herself when things
weren't quite so frantic!

❄

'Rose!'

Sue barely managed to get her greeting out before she was enveloped in a hug that was ninety per cent cashmere and ten per cent Coco Chanel perfume. She wrapped her arms around her soon-to-be mother in law and hugged her back tightly.

Sue had known Rose for years. Lucy had introduced the pair of them somewhere back in what felt like the dawn of time, and she'd always adored her friend's mum. But now, with the absence of her own parents feeling like a gaping wound, there was a lot of comfort in the fact that this wonderful woman was soon going to be an official part of her family. She was gaining a mother as well as a wife.

'Well my love, I have to say - you *do* look good,' said Rose, stepping back to survey Sue and giving her an approving nod. 'Nice and rosy - or "bright-eyed and bushy-tailed" as Lucy's father would have said!'

'Aw,' said Lucy, stepping forward and wrapping an arm around each of them, 'dear old dad.'

Rose's smile softened. 'He would be so happy to see the pair of you setting out on this adventure together, you know.'

The little catch in Rose's voice brought sudden tears to Sue's eyes and she was very glad of the warm weight of Lucy's arm around her shoulders.

'Come on,' said Lucy, 'why don't the pair of you grab a table over by the fire, and I'll make us all coffees?'

'Sounds perfect,' said Sue, smiling at her gratefully and doing her best to swallow down the swell of emotion. 'Come on Rose, let me fill you in on your daughter's scandalous behaviour while she was on her hen do!'

'Don't you dare, Sue Taylor!' said Lucy, looking horrified.

Sue winked at her. 'Okay, okay, I promise it'll be the abridged version.'

Lucy promptly stuck her tongue out at Sue, making Rose laugh. 'I wasn't ever able to get her out of the habit of doing that!'

Sue and Rose settled down at one of the tables in front of the roaring fireplace, and Rose let out a contented sigh as she leaned back.

'You okay?' said Sue, frowning slightly. 'Not too tired from your journey?'

'Don't *you* start fussing around too,' tutted Rose, giving her a little smile. 'My daughter has more than enough mother-hen instinct to cover all three of us!'

'You're right there,' laughed Sue. 'Sorry. I promise not to fuss - after I've said just one thing.'

'Okay - let's hear it,' said Rose, raising an eyebrow at her.

'Are you sure you're happy staying in the flat upstairs? There's more than enough room at my place, and you know we'd love to have you there!'

Rose shook her head, and grabbed Sue's hand across the table, covering it with both of her own.

'Thank you, but no. Any other time, I would *love* to stay with the pair of you. In fact, I'm sure you'll come to regret your rash offer because I plan to make a right old nuisance out of myself. But this time it's different. You're going to be newly-weds. And as you've decided not to disappear off on a honeymoon, you need your little love-nest all to yourselves.'

'But-'

'But nothing!' laughed Rose. 'Trust me. This is a very sweet, very special time - no matter how low-key you're playing it - and I want you both to enjoy every second of your wedding. Besides . . . I might be an old biddy, but you never know . . . I might just meet some-one. It *is* Christmas in Little Bamton after all . . . and frankly, having you two around would rather cramp my style!'

Sue bashed the table with her free hand as a surprised snort of laughter escaped her.

'What are you two giggling about?' demanded Lucy, appearing carrying three steaming cups of coffee.

'Your mum's on the pull!' chuckled Sue, wiping a stray tear from her eyes.

'Oh *you*,' muttered Rose, swatting at Sue's hand. 'I was just saying that I'm more than happy staying upstairs because I didn't want the pair of you putting any potential gentlemen callers off while I'm here, that's all.'

'Mother!' laughed Lucy.

'What? Nothing wrong with keeping an eye out for

love, is there?' said Rose, doing her best to look sweet and innocent.

'Nothing at all,' said Sue as she grabbed Lucy's hand and kissed the back of her fingers, making her blush a rosy pink.

'So, how's this all going to work then?' asked Rose. 'I mean, the night before the wedding and all that. Are you going a bit more traditional, or are you just going up to the hall together in Sue's truck and leaving the rest of us to find our own way?'

Sue raised her eyebrows at Lucy. She knew she'd been meaning to tell her mum all the details for weeks . . . but either it was one of Lucy's to-do list items that had slipped through the cracks, or Rose's memory wasn't quite the sharp tack they were used to any more.

'Well,' said Sue, deciding to jump in as soon as she saw the worried look on Lucy's face, 'I'm staying up at Bamton Hall the night before with my maid of honour, Amber, and Mark-'

'The vicar?' Rose cut in.

'Yes him - he's my best man, and he'll be joining us first thing.'

'And what about you, love?' she asked Lucy.

'I'm going to spend the night down here in the cottage. Eve, Emmy and Caro were planning on joining me in here for a bit the night before - so you can join us too if you fancy! Then they're all heading up to the hall in the morning.'

'What - in a minibus?' asked Rose.

'You know, you could always get that pink monstrosity from your hen-do back for another spin around the village!' said Sue.

'Not a chance,' laughed Lucy.

'A massive pink limo,' added Sue, seeing the look of confusion on Rose's face. 'It nearly got stuck on the bridge on the way in!'

'We had loads of fun,' said Lucy, 'but it's not got a patch on what we've got planned for the big day. Mum, you and I will be travelling up to Bamton Hall in a horse-drawn carriage!'

'Oh, how romantic,' sighed Rose. 'I can't wait. What a wonderful thing to do!'

'Sue organised it for me,' said Lucy, giving Sue the kind of soft smile that always made her feel like she was sipping on the richest hot chocolate.

'We don't have to . . . erm . . . steer the horse ourselves, do we?' asked Rose.

'No - you'll be in Alf's safe hands there,' said Sue, only just managing to tear her eyes away from Lucy.

'Alf, eh?' said Rose, one eyebrow going up. 'Is he . . . eligible?'

'Blimey mum,' chuckled Lucy, 'you're not messing around, are you?'

'How many men have their own horse-drawn carriage? He sounds like a catch to me!' said Rose.

'Well, you do have a point,' laughed Sue. 'And Thor the horse is pretty special too. You'll love him!'

'Don't encourage her,' sighed Lucy.

'Why not? And yes - Alf's eligible. A bit rough around the edges maybe, but the man's got a heart of gold and grows the best Brussel Sprouts in Devon.'

'Well - that decides things then, I'll need to make sure I've got my glad-rags on!'

'You always look gorgeous, mum,' said Lucy sincerely.

'Thank you, darling,' said Rose, beaming at her daughter. 'And on that note, I have to agree with what you said earlier too by the way - Ali looked very well.'

'Is she back at Dragonfly?' asked Sue, glancing around the pub as if she might find Ali loitering in one of the corners. She'd forgotten that Lucy'd picked her up from the station at the same time as Rose.

'Yep,' said Lucy, taking a sip of her coffee. 'She was desperate to see Emmy and Jon, but she sent her love and says she can't wait for the wedding.'

Sue nodded, then let out a little sigh. As much as she was enjoying hanging out with Lucy and her mum, the mention of Alf's Brussel sprouts had caused her thoughts to fly back up to the allotments. She wondered if they'd had any luck yet. Surely not . . . but then, if they *did* find the ring, it would be the last piece of the puzzle. She shouldn't get her hopes up though, should she?

'Sue, love,' said Rose, 'you okay there? You're miles away!'

Sue smiled and nodded. 'I'm fine,' she said, 'but I'd

better leave you two to it for a minute and start getting lunch for the lads up at the allotments.'

'I can do that for you!' said Lucy.

'I tell you what,' said Rose, getting to her feet, 'why don't you both do that together while I head upstairs and have a bit of a rest?'

'Do you need me to bring your bags up?' asked Sue, getting to her feet quickly.

'What did I tell you about the mother-hen thing?' laughed Rose. 'And no, thank you - they're already up there.'

'I'll just come up with you and check you've got everything you need,' said Lucy.

'Oh no you don't,' said Rose. 'Stay put, young lady. I'm a big girl . . . and besides, I fancy a little nap!'

Sue watched as Lucy gave her mum a quick kiss on the cheek before Rose disappeared with a backwards grin out of the front door.

'Your mum's trouble!' she said approvingly.

'Yep!' laughed Lucy. 'Now then . . . did you say something about lunches!'

Sue nodded and followed Lucy through to the pub's little kitchen. As soon as they were there though, Sue reached for her hand and pulled Lucy towards her.

'Hey,' said Sue, her voice coming out higher-pitched than usual with nerves, 'I just wanted to say . . . that I'm sorry.'

'Why?' said Lucy, going wide-eyed.

'For being . . . well . . . maybe a bit distracted?' said

Sue. 'I want you to know that nothing's more important to me than you. Nothing. And I can't wait to get married to you . . .' she trailed away, biting her lip.

'But?' said Lucy, not taking her eyes off her, though her voice wavered as if there were tears behind it.

'But I really wish my mum and dad were here,' said Sue, her voice coming out thick now. She swallowed hard, doing her best not to cry.

'I get it. I miss my dad too,' said Lucy quietly. 'I'd give anything for him to be here with us, celebrating.'

Sue nodded, unable to say anything.

'I've been scared that . . .' Lucy trailed off.

'What?

'That you'd change your mind. About getting married, I mean.'

'Never,' said Sue earnestly, stepping forwards and gently dropping a kiss on Lucy's forehead.

'Thank you,' said Lucy, letting out a long sigh. It sounded a bit like she'd been holding her breath for weeks.

'I love you, Luce,' said Sue, gently.

'I love you too,' said Lucy, squeezing her hands tight before letting out a little laugh. 'Right. Cheese toasties, you say?'

Sue smiled and nodded. 'Yep - half a dozen. Along with three teas, two hot chocolates and a coffee.'

'Coming right up,' said Lucy. 'Though I can't for the life of me figure out why this club decided on an outing to the allotments this close to Christmas!' she laughed. 'Totally random!'

Sue nodded and busied herself with grating a mound of cheese. She hated lying to Lucy about what she was up to, but she'd sworn Sam to secrecy, as well as the entire club. She didn't want to tell Lucy about the ring . . . at least, not until it was actually found. And if it wasn't, she'd just have to go and buy that band she'd picked out.

'Yeah,' said Sue at last, feeling Lucy's gaze still on her. She turned and smiled at her, willing herself to look as natural as possible. 'You know what they say though - nowt so queer as folk!'

Lucy shrugged. 'Especially metal detectorists, it seems!'

CHAPTER 9

LUCY

'Oh, my love,' said Rose, her hand flying to her mouth as Lucy answered the door to Sue's cottage for her. 'You look . . . you are . . . your dad would be in bits!'

'Do I look okay?' asked Lucy, smoothing her hands down the gorgeous velvet of her dress for what felt like the hundredth time since Emmy and Eve had helped her step into it, doing up the tiny, fiddly buttons for her before holding her hands while she'd slipped into her dark red, satin shoe-boots.

Her mum took a step back and scanned her from head to toe, and it was as much as Lucy could do not to fidget.

'More than okay, my love,' said her mum at last, 'you look absolutely beautiful.'

'Thanks, mum,' said Lucy, leaning forward and

kissing her gently on the cheek. 'Come on in,' she added, carefully shifting her skirt so that she could move back into the relative warmth of the cottage without going flying over the little puddle train. 'It's freezing out there this morning!'

She shot a quick glance at the sky before closing the door behind her mum. It had that leaden look about it that made her wonder if she might be blessed with a little flurry of snow for her wedding day.

'Are the others still here?'

'Nope,' said Lucy, following her through to the sitting room. All she wanted to do was flop down into the sofa and relax, but she didn't dare. 'Jon's just collected them and whisked them up to Bamton Hall. I'm quite glad actually, Emmy wouldn't stop fussing with my hair!' she laughed.

'Well, she's done a beautiful job on it!' said Rose, walking around her carefully to get a good look.

'I love it, actually,' said Lucy, almost shyly, doing her best to resist the temptation to run her hands over her hair again. Emmy had spent most of the morning batting her away so that she didn't ruin the do.

She couldn't believe what a nice job Emmy had done, though as her friend had pointed out, it wasn't really that different to arranging flowers if you thought about it. She'd weaved the top section with tiny white winter roses before securing the curls with two old-fashioned diamanté combs Caro had found on a buying trip. She'd left the bottom section loose so that it fell around her shoulders in bouncy ringlets.

'I have to say, I do like your shoes,' said her mum with an admiring glance down and the dark red heels poking out from under the white velvet.

'Thanks. I wanted a little touch of Christmas, you know?'

'They're very . . . you?' said her mum with a laugh. 'But I think something's missing.'

'Well,' said Lucy, nervously fingering the marcasite necklace that dangled just above her cleavage, 'my flowers are up at the hall - didn't see any point having them for the carriage ride up as we've got the sitting room up there to gather in before the ceremony.'

'I didn't mean flowers,' laughed her mum.

'I don't think there's room in this dress for anything else!' said Lucy, running her hands down over the bodice.

'Here - take a look at this and see what you think,' said her mum with a smile. She plonked her capacious handbag onto the sofa and rummaged in its depths for a moment before drawing out a squashy package wrapped in brown parcel paper and tied in the old fashioned way with string.

'What's this?'

'Why don't you open it and find out?' said her mum, raising her eyebrows in amusement.

Lucy perched gingerly on the arm of the sofa and tugged at the string until it fell away from the paper.

She gently peeled back the folds and caught a glimpse of snowy-white yarn, shot through with dark red satin.

'Oh mum!' cried Lucy, picking it gently out of the paper and shaking it so that she could see it properly.

It was a short, beautifully hand-knitted cape. The pattern along its lower edge perfectly matched the vines and snowflakes on her dress. The narrow, deep red ribbon that was threaded through the soft white yarn picked out the colour of her shoes perfectly. It was finished with a fine sprinkling of tiny, silver crystals that glittered in the light.

'Do you like it?' asked her mum.

Lucy glanced at her, desperately blinking back the happy tears that were threatening to spoil the perfect make-up Eve had applied for her earlier. 'Like it?' she whispered. 'Mum, it is one of the most beautiful things I've ever seen. Thank you so much!'

'Well,' said Rose, taking it gently from her and proceeding to throw it around her bare shoulders, tying the fastening ribbon in neat a bow, 'we don't want you to freeze before you get the chance to say "I do", do we!'

'But . . . how did you know?' said Lucy, stroking her fingers over the soft wool.

'Caro!' laughed her mum. 'You must have told her that I knit?'

Lucy nodded her head. They'd had long conversations about her mum's prowess with the knitting needles - mainly in relation to the small mountain of baby-knitting Caro had her eye on, even though she didn't know her purl from her plain.

'Well, she called me as soon as you chose your dress. I think she had a hunch that you hadn't given something as basic as warmth any thought!'

Lucy laughed. 'Well, she was right there! I'm afraid that didn't even make it onto my to-do list.'

'Thankfully, your friends are more on the ball when it comes to these practicalities, eh?' laughed Rose, rolling her eyes. 'Anyway, she sent me a picture of your shoes and your necklace after your final fitting session too, and I added the ribbons and crystals - just to tie everything in. You don't have to wear it in the actual wedding, but it should keep you warm on our way up there!'

'I think it's one of my favourite things in the whole world,' said Lucy earnestly.

'Do you want to go and have a look in the mirror - just to check that I got it right? If you don't like it, you could always just hide it in my bag before anyone sees you?'

Lucy shook her head. 'I love it,' she said. 'I don't need to see it to know that I'm wearing it all the way to the hall.' *And pretty much every day for the rest of my entire life!* she added to herself, stroking the soft knit again. She was sure she could feel her mum's love for her in every single stitch.

'Well, if you're sure . . .' said her mum, fiddling with the buttons of her own thick, deep red cashmere coat.

Lucy nodded. 'Thank you, mum,' she said, reaching across, taking her hand and giving it a squeeze.

'Right then,' said her mum, clearing her throat, 'so now we just . . . wait? For this Alf person?'

Lucy nodded. 'I'm hoping he gets here before the snow does,' she said with a nervous giggle.

'Well, if the snow does catch us on our way up there - I've got my umbrella in here, so we'll stay nice and dry,' said her mum, patting her handbag.

Lucy nodded, smiling at her mum. She was so grateful to have her by her side on her big day.

There was a knock on the front door of the cottage, and Rose bustled out of the living room at speed to answer it while Lucy gathered her long skirt and followed her mother at a more leisurely pace. The last thing she needed to do right now was trip over her dress or put a heel through the velvet before she'd even managed to get up to Bamton Hall.

She reached the open front door and then paused, watching the little scene that was unfolding just beyond the garden gate.

Alf and her mum were standing at the front of the carriage, and Alf was tipping what she knew would be Polo mints into her mother's palm. Lucy smiled as she watched her mum hold the mints out cautiously towards Thor. The stocky little silver horse snaffled them gently before chomping with his eyes closed in complete bliss.

Her mum looked like she was completely entranced, but Lucy wasn't certain whether it was by Thor, Alf or a mixture of the two of them. All she knew for sure was right at this moment, Rose Brown had completely forgotten about the bride waiting on the cottage doorstep, ready to head up to Bamton Hall for her wedding.

'Hi Alf,' said Lucy gently, not wanting to ruin the moment between them, but equally, very keen to begin their journey. The clouds above seemed to be getting darker - and her nervous butterflies were beginning to flap their wings uncomfortably under the bodice of her dress.

'Oh, Lucy lass,' gasped Alf, tearing his eyes away from her mother and finally catching sight of her waiting by the garden gate. He whipped the cap off his head and beamed at her. 'You look absolutely beautiful!'

Lucy grinned at him as he came towards her and then he took her by surprise by reaching up and cupping her cheek, just like her dad used to do when she was a little girl.

'Just the most beautiful bride I've ever seen!' he said gruffly.

'Thank you!' said Lucy. She could feel her face flushing with pleasure. She adored Alf, and even though she couldn't have her dad by her side today, she couldn't imagine anyone better to accompany her and her mum on this little trip. She leaned forward and kissed him lightly on his bristly cheek as he patted her gently.

'Hello Thor, lad!' said Lucy, pulling back from Alf and smiling at the little horse. Normally she would have given Thor a big hug too, but she decided that had better wait until after the ceremony - just in case he decided he liked the look of white velvet as much as he enjoyed polos.

'Did you ladies want a photo outside the cottage before we all set off?' asked Alf.

'Oh blimey,' said Lucy, covering her mouth in horror. 'I *knew* I'd forgotten something!'

'What is it dear?' asked her mum, raising her eyebrows. 'I can nip back to the cottage . . .'

'I don't think you'll find a professional photographer in there,' said Lucy. She couldn't believe it - it wasn't that she'd managed to skip over this vital point when she'd been working through her to-do lists - she'd missed putting it on the list in the first place.

'Don't worry about that now, lass,' said Alf. 'Look!' he yanked a surprisingly snazzy iPhone from his waistcoat pocket and waggled it at her. 'This day and age, every man and his horse has got one of these - we'll just have to ask everyone to snap away to their heart's content and you'll have more photos than you can shake a stick at!'

Lucy let out a huge sigh and nodded. 'I guess you're right.'

'Of course he is,' said her mum, shooting a grateful smile at Alf. 'I'll send Caro a text as soon as we set off to make sure she spreads the word.'

'Okay. Thanks, mum. And yes please, Alf - I'd love a photo of me, mum and Thor . . . though I don't want to get too close in case he decides to give my dress a grassy nibble,' she laughed.

'Don't worry about that - I'll give him another polo to keep him busy!'

As soon as Alf had fired off a bunch of shots of her and her mum on either side of Thor, followed by selfies with the four of them posing together because her mum thought "they'd be fun" - Alf handed them both up into the carriage and made sure they were snuggled up under a red, tartan blanket, ready for the ride.

'Trot on, Thor lad!' called Alf from the front. 'Trot on, boy!' And with a lurch, they set off towards the hall.

Lucy grabbed her mum's hand and gave it a squeeze, turning to her with tears in her eyes.

'Thank you,' she said.

'What for, lovely?' asked her mum, surprised.

'Everything,' she said simply. 'I just feel so lucky to have you here with me.'

'Well,' said her mum gently, 'that goes for both of us. And thank *you* too!'

'What for?' echoed Lucy.

'Well . . . for bringing a man with a horse-drawn

carriage into my life, of course!' she said, her face completely serious.

Lucy stared at her a moment, then, as the first flakes of snow floated gently down to greet them, they both started to giggle.

CHAPTER 10

SUE

Sue watched Thor jog to a halt on the sweeping patch of gravel outside the main entrance to the West Wing of Bamton Hall. She knew she should go back inside - or at the very least, she should turn away. Wasn't it supposed to be bad luck for her to see the bride before the ceremony, or some such nonsense? But then - she was bride number two, so she wasn't one hundred per cent certain whether it counted in this instance.

Besides, she was tucked away in amongst the guests' cars - no one would notice her over here. She'd had to duck when Scarlet and Davy had come running out – hopping into Scarlet's car and disappearing at speed - but other than that, she hadn't seen a soul until the carriage had arrived. She just wanted to catch one last glimpse of Lucy before she headed off.

She knew there was a good chance that she might

regret what she was about to do - but she *had* to do it. She couldn't go to her own wedding without doing this first. The last thing she wanted to do was hurt Lucy or cause her a second of doubt - but she didn't feel like she had a choice in the matter right now. Her heart felt like it was breaking, and she had to try - one last time - to make it whole again.

Sue watched as Alf made his way around the side of the carriage, holding his hand up to help Rose down first. Then she saw Lucy throw a blanket off her lap and get to her feet.

Sue gasped. Maybe it had been a bad idea to wait and watch after all - but she had to make sure that Lucy was inside the hall itself before she made her dash for it. She couldn't risk being caught mid disappearing-act. That would be a total disaster.

But how could she leave now? She felt like some kind of spell had been cast over her as she watched her beautiful bride-to-be step down onto the gravel with a flash of deepest red from her shoes. She looked like . . . like . . . Sue couldn't put it into words. All she knew was that she couldn't look away from this wonderful woman who held her whole heart in her hands. There was some kind of magic at work. Sue gazed at Lucy, half wishing she would turn and spot her over here in her uncomfortable hiding place - and half dreading it at the same time.

Sue watched as Lucy straightened out her dress and peered up at the sky for a moment. Then she took her mother's arm and strode towards the double doors of the hall. Alf hopped back up into the carriage and he and Thor disappeared around the back of the building.

The moment Sue saw Lucy disappear through the doors, the strange spell that had held her captivated seemed to break. Sue suddenly felt cold all over as she watched little white flakes drift down onto the gravel where Lucy had stood just moments before. She gave herself a little shake. She had to do this. She *had* to.

Moving quickly, she turned the key in the ignition of her truck, and with one last nervous glance back towards the doors of Bamton Hall to make sure there was no one there to see her leaving, she pulled out of the car park and turned onto the tree-lined driveway.

The moment she pulled out onto the road, Sue took a deep breath and did her best to relax her shoulders. They'd been hovering somewhere up near her ears ever since she'd got out of bed, but now that she'd decided on her course of action she needed to try to relax a bit.

The problem was it was a bit like fighting a losing battle. Her mind was racing and adrenalin was surging through her veins. After all, she *had* just walked away from her own wedding mere minutes before it was due to kick off.

Sue took another deep breath and rolled her shoulders slightly without taking her eyes off the narrow lane. The last thing she needed was to end up in a ditch like Caro had last Christmas - especially as there wasn't a living soul who had a clue where she was right now.

Plus - in her hurry to make a break for it, she'd managed to leave her mobile phone in her bedroom back at the hall. Ah well - it wasn't like she was going to need it.

As she shifted gear and swung the old truck carefully out of a narrow junction to head back towards the heart of Little Bamton, Sue's mind wandered back to the devastating conversation she'd had with Gerald and Harry after they'd finished their search of the allotments. They didn't have the news she'd been hoping for.

Gerald had greeted her with a sombre expression, and she'd known straight away that they hadn't had any luck when it came to her mum's ring. In fact, all they'd managed to find other than an assortment of ancient nails, ring-pulls and the occasional metal peg they used to pin down agricultural fleece were two, chunky cartwheel pennies dating from the seventeen-hundreds, and a rusty and slightly bent horseshoe.

They'd been incredibly apologetic about the fact that they hadn't turned up the ring, but Sue had put on a bright smile and done her best to laugh it off. The guys had all elected to hand the two old pennies and the horseshoe over to Sue as "tokens of good luck", or at least that's what Harry had said. Sue had shaken his hand and thanked them all warmly before they'd headed home, but she'd been left behind feeling about as trampled as the allotments looked. It had been her last hope, and now that was gone.

Sue took one hand off the wheel of the truck and drew out one of the heavy cartwheel pennies that she'd been carrying around with her ever since. She gripped the smooth metal tightly in her fist for a moment, trying to talk some kind of sense into herself.

What on earth was she thinking? The guys had given the allotment a thorough going over by all accounts - even the grassy verges and the ditch right at the far boundary had been searched. Her mum's ring was now officially, and permanently, lost.

So why was she in her truck heading back to the allotments when she should be standing under the decorated archway waiting to marry Lucy? She didn't really have an answer for that - but from the moment she'd woken up that morning, she'd known that it was what she needed to do. Even after the hours and hours she'd spent on the allotments in the years since she'd lost the ring, somehow, today, she needed one last visit. She needed to say goodbye.

It felt really strange to be pulling the truck into the empty pub car park. Sue came to a stop and killed the engine. The place was closed for the day - with a cheerful sign on the door announcing the wedding, apologising for any inconvenience and inviting everyone to come back for Christmas Eve drinks before the Carol service tomorrow evening.

Sue hopped out of the truck. She needed to get this done. She strode out into the village square and avoided looking around her just in case anyone caught her eye and demanded an explanation as to why she was here rather than up at Bamton Hall saying her vows.

Heading up the little track that lead towards the allotments, she paused to heave the five-barred gate open just wide enough for her to squeeze through. Sue trudged in the borrowed wellies that she'd half-inched from Horace's boot room, walking right up to the top of the plot before turning to look around her. Now that she was here, she wasn't really sure why she'd come - other than that deep in her bones, she knew that it was important for her to be here right now.

She knew it was ridiculous to think that she stood any kind of a chance of finding the missing ring now - not after half a dozen very experienced men with some seriously technical equipment hadn't had any luck after hours spent searching. Sue let out a long, slow breath, watching as a few lazy snowflakes swirled around her, almost like they were dancing rather than falling.

Sue turned the big old penny in her fingers as she stared around her, wondering what she was really doing here – what she was waiting for. The worn metal had warmed where she'd been gripping it in her hand for so long.

'If you are a lucky penny,' she whispered, 'help me find that ring.'

She stared down at the tufty grass at her feet and then let out a bitter laugh. As if it would be that easy! Who was she even kidding?

Suddenly she knew exactly why she was here. It wasn't to find the ring after all. It was to say one last goodbye to her mum and dad. She couldn't carry this weight of sadness into her new life with Lucy. She needed to let it go.

'Mum?' she said in a low, quivering voice. 'Dad? Can you hear me?' She peered around her. Was she looking for some kind of sign? Maybe. But either way, she was going to say what she'd come to say. 'I really miss you both,' she said, her voice breaking. 'I'm meant to be marrying my best friend today . . . and I just can't face it . . . not without you both with me.'

Sue paused, rubbing hard at her face, doing her best to wipe away the tears that had started pouring down her cheeks, leaving freezing tracks in the cold December air. She took in a deep, shuddering breath and felt in her jeans pocket for a hanky. Pulling out a slightly tatty square of kitchen roll, she blew her nose, trying to calm herself.

She closed her eyes for a moment, willing the tears to stop. When she opened them again, her attention was caught by a flickering movement out of the corner of her eye. Turning slowly, she spotted a little robin perched on the handle of the fork she'd left standing in the carrots - ready to lift them tomorrow in time for Christmas day.

'Hello, you,' she said, giving the little bird a watery smile as it regarded her with bright interest. 'How did you know I needed a bit of company, eh?' she said, her voice catching slightly.

The robin shifted, angling its head this way and that, clearly wondering why she wasn't busy digging up some worms for its dinner. As she watched it, its feathers puffed up against the chill, the memory of working with her old dad in his own vegetable patch when she was tiny came back to her. He'd always whistled to the robin when it visited. It had been so used to him that it would follow him along the patch as he worked, just a few feet away from where he was digging or weeding, yanking out worms from the newly-turned earth.

As she watched, another robin appeared, landing on the handle next to the first.

'Is that your wife?' said Sue, a delighted smile spreading across her face. The second bird ducked and bobbed, and then turned to stare straight at her too. It made her think of her mum - who'd appear with a cup of tea for her dad in a fine bone china cup, two rich tea biscuits resting in the saucer. She'd always tut about the muddy fingerprints he'd leave behind when he was finished, but there was always so much love in that little tut. So much familiarity and joy.

Sue glanced down at the coin still in her hand and then back at the two little birds who were still watching her intently. Well, she'd been hoping for some kind of Christmas miracle. She'd thought she'd lost her last link to her parents on the day that ring had slipped from her neck. But of course she hadn't. She had years and years of precious memories just like this - she just needed to open her heart to them.

'Thank you,' she whispered to the birds. It felt like they'd just given her the best wedding present ever. 'Do you want to see the ring I picked out for Lucy?' she asked. The birds bobbed and one cocked his head as if listening. Sue smiled. She wasn't sure if she was talking to the robins or her parents by this point . . . but she wasn't sure it really mattered either.

Reaching into her pocket, she drew out the little octagonal, red velvet box. Slowly and carefully so as not to scare them, Sue flipped open the top and held it out towards them. 'What do you reckon?'

The first robin hopped down into the carrot patch and started picking through the brown stems, but the second stayed watching her.

Sue glanced down at the gold band and sighed. It still wasn't the ring she'd dreamed of placing on Lucy's finger today, but maybe that wasn't what was important.

'I need to go,' she said, closing the box and popping it back in her pocket along with the penny. 'Mum, dad - I love you both so much. I miss you. But I'm happy. I've found someone I love like you two loved each other. You'd really like her. She's kind and beautiful and . . . she's my other half.'

As she stopped speaking, both robins suddenly took flight, and as they reached the relative shelter of the bare hazel hedge the snow started to flurry down from the sky in earnest.

'Time to go,' breathed Sue.

She took a couple of steps towards the gate but then turned back towards the carrot patch again. Snowflakes were already beginning to settle on the rough ground. She paused, thinking hard. If this carried on the whole allotment could be under a thick, white blanket by the morning - and there would be no chance of digging up the carrots for Christmas dinner.

'Okay - quick change of plan,' she muttered, grabbing the fork and beginning to dig. She'd quickly lift enough for Christmas and pop them in the back of her truck.

It didn't take Sue long to lift a good pile. She looked at them for a moment and decided that maybe a couple more would be a good idea . . . just in case. She thrust the fork in the ground again and wiggled it until she could wrap her cold, muddy fingers around the top of the next few carrots. Just as she was pulling the last one loose, one of the robins reappeared and fluttered down onto the newly-dug earth mere inches away from her hands.

'Oh my,' laughed Sue in delight. 'Hello again!'

The robin hopped a couple of inches closer, and then landed on one of the carrots she was in the process of lifting.

'You *are* a cheeky blighter,' she laughed, pausing so as not to scare it. It pecked a couple of times at the soil covering the carrot, which crumbled away, and then it took flight again. This time, Sue didn't follow its movement as far as the hedge, she was too busy staring at the carrot in her hands.

'It can't be,' she gasped, running a shaking thumb over the surface of the carrot to wipe away more mud. There, halfway down the length of the root, partly grown in, was a wide gold band with a small, grubby ruby just about visible.

CHAPTER 11

LUCY

'There she is!' grinned Emmy, as Lucy followed her mum into the sitting room that had been set aside for her, her mum and her bridesmaids to use before the ceremony.

'Oh Luce,' breathed Caro, getting to her feet with some difficulty and coming over to her. 'Look at that cape!'

'Mum made it for me,' beamed Lucy, stroking her fingers over the knit for the thousandth time since she'd put it on.

'Wow Rose - you're one seriously talented lady!' said Caro with evident awe in her voice.

'You knew I was making it,' laughed her mum, shaking her head at Caro's enthusiasm. 'You sent me all those photos, for goodness sake!'

'I had no idea you could make something like this

though,' said Caro, reaching out a finger and tracing it up one of the ribbons towards a crystal bead.

'Oi,' laughed Lucy, 'that tickles, birthday girl!'

'Oops, sorry,' said Caro with a smile.

'Is it your birthday?' asked Rose. 'I wish I'd have known - I would have made you something.'

'In that case, I wish you'd known too,' said Caro with a grin.

'Well, happy birthday,' said Rose, gathering a surprised Caro up in a motherly hug.

'It's not just Caro's birthday, Rose,' said Eve, coming over to hug Lucy. 'It's the anniversary of her crash landing into Little Bamton too!'

'I heard all about that,' said Rose, 'not a good birthday, eh?'

'Actually,' said Caro, resting a gentle hand on her belly, 'it was the best birthday I've ever had.'

'Until today, of course,' said Lucy with a grin.

'Exactly! Today gives us the excuse for joint anniversary and birthday parties for life,' she grinned, taking Lucy's hand and leading her over towards the squashy sofa.

'What time is it,' asked Lucy as she sank into the cushions, and promptly tried to sit up straighter to stop her dress from getting creased. 'Surely it's nearly time . . .?'

Eve glanced at her watch. 'Not long - maybe about five minutes. But we can all just relax - Amber's going to come and let us know when everyone's in place.'

'I know what I meant to ask you, Luce,' said Emmy, clearly trying to distract her and stop her from turning into a nervous wreck while they waited.

'Oh yes?' she said, raising an eyebrow and hoping against hope that Emmy wasn't about to give away any details of her rather rowdy hen-night in front of her mum.

'Yeah - what music have you chosen to have for our grand entrance? I mean, you guys decided to do without a rehearsal, so I-'

'Balls!' squeaked Lucy as an icy feeling tricked down her spine.

'Lucy!' said her mum, laughing.

'I . . . I forgot to sort out any music!' she said, looking around at her friends in horror.

'But . . . how?!' said Caro in surprise.

'The same way I'd have ended up without a dress if it wasn't for you!' said Lucy, doing her best not to panic and failing miserably.

'Well, now's not the time to worry about it,' said her mum firmly. 'This wedding will be absolutely beautiful – and keeping things simple can be very powerful.'

Lucy nodded and grabbing her mum's hand, she gave it a grateful squeeze. She'd had her heart set on walking down the aisle to Pachelbel's Canon. Sure, it was a cliché, but she adored that piece of music.

'What would you have chosen, Luce?' asked Eve.

'Pachelbel's Canon,' she muttered, giving a little shrug, trying to cover just how gutted she felt right now. She wished she hadn't just caught the look that passed between Emmy, Eve and Caro . . . one that clearly said, "what else has she forgotten?!"

'If you're wondering what else I've forgotten,' said Lucy with a wry smile, 'that'd be any kind of photographer.'

'We've already sorted that out,' said Eve, as Emmy dragged out her phone and started to fiddle with it.

'Eh? How?' asked Lucy in surprise.

'Well, your mum texted Caro to give us the heads up, so Davy's nipped back over to our place to grab his camera - he's pretty good, you know - so as well as everyone being under strict instructions to act like a bunch of smart-phone paparazzi, Davy's going to get some more formal shots for you too.'

'What a hero!' said Lucy. 'Eve - thank you!'

'Don't thank me,' she laughed, 'it was his idea. Scarlet drove herself up here, so she gave him a lift . . . they *should* be back by now, but I don't want to think too much about what those two might have got up to with a few minutes alone!'

'Like that, is it?' giggled Emmy, pocketing her phone again.

'You could say that. They've been spending rather a lot of time together!' laughed Eve.

'Well,' said Lucy, 'Scarlet's a lovely girl. I can just see the pair of them hitting it off!'

'Oh, they've done that alright,' said Eve, rolling her eyes.

'Ah, young love,' said Emmy, 'so sweet, so incredibly . . . messy!'

'Eew,' laughed Caro. 'I don't want to think about that, thanks!'

'I'll second that,' said Eve with an exaggerated shudder.

The room fell silent for a moment, and Lucy had to fight the urge to start fidgeting with her dress and her hair. If she was honest, she didn't really want to be sitting here on this sofa right now, gossiping about her Saturday girl's burgeoning love life. As much as she adored spending time with her friends and her mum, all she wanted to do right at this moment was walk down the aisle towards Sue. Now she was here, she couldn't wait to get on with it. This waiting around was starting to drive her mad.

'Goodness,' said her mum, glancing at her watch.

'What?' asked Lucy, a little shiver of irrational fear weaving through her.

'Oh, nothing love,' said her mum quickly. 'I just wonder what's taking them so long to get themselves settled?'

'I could go and find out what the hold-up is if you'd like?' said Emmy.

'How late are we running?' asked Lucy. She felt a bit cut-off from reality without her watch on her wrist or her phone in her hand. It was a peculiarly helpless feeling, and she wasn't sure she liked it all that much. The excitement she'd felt in the carriage on her way up here

- so full of hope and longing and wishes for the future - somehow felt like it was starting to curdle. The longer she stayed here in this room, the worse it was getting.

'I think we're . . . erm . . .' Caro glanced at her own watch then over at Eve. Lucy couldn't miss the worried look that flashed between the pair of them.

'About twenty minutes late at the moment, lovely,' said Eve gently. 'I'm sure it's nothing - probably just an AWOL guest, or maybe the terrible two have managed to bulldoze some of the decorations or something.'

Lucy had to crack a smile at that. 'Yeah - now that's actually more than likely!' she said with a relieved chuckle as an image of the pair of naughty Labradors on a rampage through the library crossed her mind's eye. She'd been adamant that pets were allowed - even encouraged - at the ceremony. She knew Sue had included personal invitations to Finn's dog, Wilf, and both Tarmac and Diesel too. Suddenly she wasn't so sure that had been such a great plan after all.

When Amber still hadn't appeared to summon them all ten minutes later, however, Lucy decided to take Emmy up on her offer and asked her to go and find out what the hold-up was.

Lucy was now pacing the length of the room in an attempt to stem her nerves. The others were chatting away about her mum's various knitting projects in an attempt to keep things light and easy, but by this point, they weren't fooling anyone. Lucy wasn't an idiot. She knew that a delay of more than thirty minutes couldn't be a good sign. She just couldn't wrap her head around what the hold-up might be. If it *did* turn out to be the dogs, she'd definitely be withholding their treats next time she saw them as payback for scaring her!

She'd just about decided that it was time for her to follow Emmy and go and investigate things for herself when the door creaked open and Emmy came back in, followed by a very pale and troubled looking Amber.

Lucy's heart flipped and her hand went instinctively to her chest. Eve materialised at her side and put an arm around her, and Lucy leaned into the silent comfort. Something terrible had happened, she just knew it.

'Lucy, lovely,' said Emmy, walking towards her.

'What?' said Lucy. Her voice sounded strangled, and she cleared her throat in an attempt to sound more normal. 'What's happened?' she tried again, but this time it just came out high pitched and squeaky.

Her mum appeared on her other side and took her hand.

'Amber?' said Lucy quietly, appealing to her more blunt nature as Emmy seemed to be struggling to get the words out.

'It's Sue,' said Amber slowly.

'Is she okay?' said Lucy, her voice wavering. 'What's happened? Is she ill? I need to see her!'

'Luce,' said Amber, her firm but gentle tone just

about managing to penetrate the waves of panic that were crashing over her. 'We can't find Sue.'

'What?' breathed Lucy, shaking her head.

She felt her mum's hand tighten around hers.

'Her truck's gone from the car park,' said Emmy gently. 'We're not sure where she's gone, or why. But she isn't at Bamton Hall.'

'There's got to be some kind of simple explanation.'

Lucy was pretty sure that it was her mum who'd just spoken, but right now, it was as much as she could do to stay on her feet. Sue was . . . gone? Had her strange sense of foreboding not been quite so irrational after all?

'I don't understand,' said Caro. 'Sue wouldn't just leave without saying something to someone. It's just not *her!*'

Lucy shrugged. Grief made people do strange things. Running out on your own wedding might be one of them.

'She probably just forgot something and dashed back to the village to get it,' said Eve.

'You're right,' said her mum, nodding and giving Lucy's hand another squeeze.

Lucy knew what they were doing. They were trying to bolster her. Trying to lift her up and give her hope. But right at this moment, it felt like her entire world was on the verge of crashing down around her ears. She wanted to shout and scream. Instead, she gently disentangled herself from Caro, let go of her mum's hand and walked slowly towards the door. She needed air.

'Lucy, love . . .' called her mum.

Lucy didn't pause. She headed out through the sitting room door and headed down the hallway, gathering speed - only to crash straight into Sam as he pelted around the corner.

'Oof!' he grunted, catching her before she stumbled.

'Sam . . . sorry . . . I . . .' Lucy was desperately fighting back tears. 'Excuse me, I-'

'Oh no you don't,' he said gently, not letting go of her shoulders.

'Sam, I need some air.'

'Then breathe,' he said gently. 'Sue's back.'

All the air seemed to rush out of Lucy's lungs at once, and she felt herself go slightly limp for a second as Sam wrapped his arm around her to hold her up.

'Come on, beautiful bride,' he said. 'Let's get you back in that room for a minute.'

Lucy didn't have the energy to fight him, so she let Sam lead her straight back into the sitting room.

'Sam!' Caro gasped, as he helped Lucy onto the sofa. 'What on earth's happening?'

'Sue's back,' he said.

Lucy glanced up at him, and though the tingling void where the panic had been just moments before, she managed to take in that he was smiling.

'Is she okay?' asked Amber, frowning.

Sam nodded as Caro sank down into the sofa next to Lucy, reaching for her hand.

There was a knock at the door, and they all turned to stare. Lucy half-expected to see Sue herself standing there, but it was Mark.

'Sue asked me to deliver a message,' he said, coming over to stand in front of Lucy, his hands behind his back.

'Is she okay?' asked Lucy. She knew she'd already asked it, but right now, knowing that Sue - her best friend, her other half, the love of her life - was okay was the most important thing in the world. The wedding, the ceremony and everything else didn't even come close.

'She's fine. She wanted me to give you this,' he said, pulling a bouquet from behind his back and holding it towards her, though not close enough for her to actually take.

'What on earth?' said Eve, peering at the random bunch in Mark's hands.

Lucy frowned and leaned forward to get a better look without getting too close. At first glance, she'd thought it was flowers, but now she could see that it was carrots - freshly dug and still slightly grubby carrots - along with a few bits of dried grass, holly, teasles and mistletoe. It was all bound together with a length of garden twine.

'I don't understand,' said Lucy, letting out a noise that was half sob, half-laugh.

'Sue says she'll explain everything - but she wants you to know that she loves you and she's sorry if she scared you.'

Lucy nodded. 'So where is she?'

'Waiting under the archway for her bride,' said Mark with a gentle smile.

CHAPTER 12

SUE

'Thank G . . . erm . . . goodness you're back,' stuttered Sue the minute Mark came into view around the corner. She'd been doing her best to ignore the muttering of their guests drifting out from behind the closed library door as she'd paced the hallway outside. Clearly, everyone in there had had enough of waiting quietly, but right now she didn't care. All she could think about was Lucy.

'What did she say?' Sue demanded. 'Is she okay? Are we doing this or have I messed everything up?'

'Of course you're doing this,' said Mark, patting her arm in a vague attempt to get her to calm down. 'She was pretty upset - she thought you'd done a runner.'

'Why would she think that?' said Sue, her heart squeezing in her chest.

'You *are* over half an hour late to your own wedding . . . and none of us knew where you were. When we discovered that your truck was gone, I'm afraid . . . well . . . Emmy and Amber had just told Lucy the news when you reappeared!'

'Poor Luce!' said Sue. 'I feel so bad - but it was something I had to do!'

Mark nodded. 'I'm sure she'll understand as long as you explain everything to her. She loves you deeply, you know.'

'I don't know how I got so lucky,' said Sue, shaking her head and picking at the dirt that was still caked around her fingernails. She'd been in such a hurry to get back, hoping against hope that there was a chance Lucy might not even be aware that she'd been missing. Other than giving her hands a cursory rinse and quickly changing out of her tatty jeans and jumper into her wedding gear, she hadn't given the rest of her appearance much thought.

'Where in the *ruddy hell* were you?!' demanded Amber, stomping around the corner, striding straight up to her and giving her a hefty poke in the shoulder.

'Oi!' laughed Sue.

'Oi yourself,' said Amber, bristling. 'You just knocked about ten years off my life there, missus. I swear I only agreed to be your maid of honour because I thought you'd be easy-peasy - no drama - no fuss. But *noooo!* You had to go and scare everyone silly!'

'I think we should all calm ourselves a little,' said Mark in a low, soothing tone.

'I'm sorry,' said Sue, 'I really am. I just needed to . . . to say goodbye to my parents.'

'You went to the effing allotments, didn't you?' said Amber, looking like she was struggling not to roll her eyes.

Sue nodded.

'That's what that weird-arse bouquet you just sent to Lucy was about, wasn't it?'

Sue nodded again, a smile spreading over her face.

'What on *earth* are you looking so happy about?' demanded Amber. 'I'm *this* close to kicking your arse for scaring Lucy like that.'

'I found what I was looking for,' said Sue with a little shrug.

'What - the chance to say goodbye?' asked Mark.

Sue shook her head. 'No. I did go there to make my peace and try to say goodbye, but instead - I found my parents again. In here,' she said, bringing her hand up to her chest.

Mark beamed at her, but Amber was too busy staring at her filthy fingernails in horror to catch on to the importance of what she'd just said.

'Tell me you didn't do a spot of digging while you were at it?' she demanded.

'Oh. Erm, yeah,' said Sue, dropping her hand and shoving it into the pocket of her wide, bottle green trousers, wrapping her fingers around the precious cargo she'd stowed there. 'It started snowing quite hard while I was there, so I thought . . . Christmas lunch, you know . . .'

'You're impossible,' laughed Amber, throwing her hands in the air. 'Come on, I think we'd better go in, don't you?'

Sue nodded.

'Oh,' said Mark, 'did you want me to hold on to the ring for you until it's time?'

Sue thought for a moment, then shook her head. 'If you don't mind, I want Lucy to be the first one to see it.'

Mark shrugged. 'Of course.'

The heavy wooden door to the library suddenly opened and a chorus of chattering voices spilled out as Jon poked his head into the corridor.

'Are you lot coming in or not?' he demanded. 'I promised Emmy that I'd text her when everything's ready. They've waited long enough, don't you think?'

Sue nodded. 'Send that message,' she said with a grin. 'We're good to go.'

Jon gave her the thumbs up and disappeared back inside.

'Here goes nothing,' said Sue, leading the way down the aisle under the tunnel of flowers. She could feel all eyes on her as she went, but Sue kept her focus on the view of Bamton Hall's grounds spread out in front of her. Snow was now drifting down out of the sky in thick, swirling eddies. It wouldn't be long before the scene out there turned completely white. Pretty fitting for a wedding, she thought with a grin.

As she came to a halt under the archway, a short woman in a pretty floral dress got to her feet from the front row of chairs and joined her. It was Fiona, their registrar.

'I'm sorry I kept you waiting for so long,' said Sue.

'It's not a problem,' said Fiona in a deep, soothing voice. 'Is everything okay?'

'More than okay,' said Sue with a soft smile.

'And we're okay to proceed?' Fiona asked carefully.

Sue quickly turned to glance at Mark and Amber. There they were, two of her best friends - standing with her, supporting her. She raised her eyebrows at them and they both nodded, grinning back.

'We're ready,' said Sue, a swoop of nerves running through her. She peeped towards the window again and caught a quick dart of movement on the sill - it was a robin. It stood there for the briefest moment, staring right back at her before bobbing and then fluttering away across the snowy grounds.

Yes. She really was ready.

Lucy

'Are you ready, love?' asked her mum, reaching up to brush a stray hair off her forehead.

Lucy smiled and glanced over her shoulder at Caro, Emmy and Eve. 'You girls ready?'

'Born ready,' Caro grinned back at her as Emmy and Eve nodded.

'Then I am too,' said Lucy. 'Let's do this. Let's get me married.'

'At last,' chuckled her mum as she gently took Lucy's arm and tucked it into the crook of her own.

Jon stood in the doorway to the library, holding it wide open for them all. He was grinning from ear to ear as he watched them.

'After you, beautiful bridesmaids,' breathed Lucy. Eve lead the way, briefly touching her on the arm as she walked past. Emmy did the same, and then Caro leaned in and kissed her lightly on the cheek.

'Love you, Luce,' she whispered, and then followed the other two into the library.

As Lucy watched three of her best friends float serenely through the admiring crowd, she shook her head. Her mind must be playing tricks on her after all the excitement because she was sure she could hear faint music. What on earth? Had the shock actually addled her brain?

'You okay, love?' asked her mum, peering at her with a concerned look on her face. She was trying to gently move Lucy forward towards the doorway, but Lucy remained completely still, her ears pricked.

'Can you hear music?' she asked.

Her mum gave her a naughty grin, followed by a

shrug. 'I don't know,' she said, fooling no one in the process. 'Let's go in and see, shall we?'

Lucy nodded, and at last let her mum lead her to the doorway. The minute they stepped through, everyone rose to their feet, and Lucy gasped. She paused again, trying to take it all in. This was the first time she'd been in here in weeks - and it had been transformed beyond her wildest dreams.

Instead of just the simple willow arch in front of the windows that she'd been expecting, the entire aisle was decorated with sweeping arches and the spiralling willow patterns made it feel like she was walking through a woodland glade. The whole thing was decorated with holly and winter roses. From every joint in the woven willow dangled a crystal prism which caught the light and threw dancing rainbows across her path.

Her eyes went to the far end of the aisle, and suddenly she was held captive by the gaze of someone so dear and so familiar, it brought the swell of tears to her eyes. It was her Sue - looking beautiful in wide, dark-green trousers and a cream bodice shot through with gold. Her hair had been twisted into an elaborate style, and yet she still looked wild. Untamed. Free.

Lucy gripped her mum's arm more tightly and as they began the slow walk through the tunnel of flowers and rainbows together. She became aware of the tinkling music again and this time it was unmistakable. Pachelbel's Canon. She glanced around until she spotted Will perched on a wooden chair off to one side of the front arch, a classical guitar resting on his lap as he picked out every single note to perfection.

At last, they reached the front, and as they came to a halt Lucy turned to her mother and wrapped her in a proper hug. There would be none of those polite, lady-like affairs here. This was her wedding after all, and if she wanted to give her mum a cuddle that told her exactly how much she was loved, she bloody well would.

Eventually, her mum gently pulled away, giving her one last tender pat on her cheek before turning to sit in her designated spot in the front row - right next to a beaming Alf.

Lucy turned slowly and at last, came face-to-face with Sue, who was gazing at her as if she'd never seen her before.

'Hi,' said Lucy shyly, raising a few titters from the crowd.

'Hey,' said Sue with a smile. 'You look . . . unbelievable.'

'You too,' whispered Lucy, 'though you've got a little something . . .' she reached forward and brushed her thumb gently over Sue's cheek, wiping at a smear of what looked suspiciously like mud.

'Are we ready?' asked the registrar gently.

Lucy raised her eyebrows at Sue in silent question, wanting her to take the lead.

'Absolutely,' said Sue, not taking her eyes off Lucy's.

'Me too,' said Lucy with a smile.

She did her best to take everything in and listen to the beautiful words as the registrar spoke about leading their lives entwined together, but Lucy was completely captivated by Sue, unable to tear her eyes away.

'I believe you've both prepared some vows?' asked the registrar at last, and Lucy felt herself surface as if from a trance.

'I have,' said Sue. 'Or, I had. With a little help from a very talented writer,' Lucy saw her throw a grateful glance at Finn, 'I thought I had the perfect words to say to you.'

Lucy swallowed nervously, and Sue leaned forward and gently took her hand.

'Instead,' Sue continued, 'I want to tell you what happened. Why we are running so late.' Sue paused and took a deep breath. 'I felt like I needed my parents - my family - here with us in this room to be able to give myself to you fully - heart and soul. I went in search of even the tiniest sign - a hint of them I could bring here with me. And I found it.

'As I stood in Little Bamton's allotments, a memory came back to me. It was like the most precious gift, and I realised that the people you truly love are never very far away. You just have to look for them - and remember. So today, I give myself to you, body, heart and soul. You are my other half, Lucy. My family. And I love you.'

'I love you too,' murmured Lucy, fighting the lump of emotion in her throat.

'Lucy?' prompted the registrar.

'How do I follow that?' It came out as half-laugh, half-sob, but as a giggle ran through their guests, Lucy took a deep breath and smiled at Sue.

'I had a poem prepared,' she said with a tiny break in her voice, 'but it doesn't say everything I want to say to you. There *is* no way to say everything I want to say to you. There aren't enough hours left in this lifetime to tell you how much I love you. Like you said - body, heart and soul. You are my family, and I will never be far away.'

Lucy felt Sue's fingers tighten around hers and fought hard to keep her tears in check.

'You have the rings?' asked the registrar quietly.

She didn't want to be parted from Sue for a second, but Lucy let go of her hand and turned as Eve stepped forward to hand her Sue's ring. She turned back to face Sue and gasped in surprise.

Sue was holding a carrot.

Lucy blinked hard, wondering again if the stress of the morning had finally got to her. But no. She wasn't hallucinating. Sue really *was* holding a carrot.

'I wanted to show you how I found it,' said Sue, as Lucy took a step forward and she peered at the slightly grubby vegetable along with a very surprised registrar.

'Well I never!' she gasped, staring at the gold band halfway down its length.

Sue grinned up at the woman and then back at Lucy. 'It's my mum's lost wedding ring. It started snowing while I was down there, so I thought I'd better dig some carrots for Christmas lunch.'

Lucy felt her lips twitch with amusement. At least this explained the streak of mud on her blushing bride's cheek!

'Anyway, I was about to stop when a robin landed on this one, pecked away some of the mud and revealed this. I always wanted you to have mum's ring.'

Lucy watched, completely breathless, as Sue gripped both ends of the gnarly carrot in her hands. With some effort, she snapped it in half before sliding the gold band free.

Mark promptly stepped forward, and handing Sue a handkerchief from his pocket, he took the mangled pieces of carrot from her as she proceeded to clean the remaining mud from the ring.

'Well I never!' said the registrar again, eliciting a giggle from those watching. Then she visibly pulled herself together. 'Erm, right. Sue, repeat after me,' she said. 'I give you this ring as a token of my love-'

Sue stared deep into Lucy's eyes as she repeated the words, one hand gently holding hers.

'And a symbol of our shared life together,' continued the registrar.

'And a symbol of our shared life together,' repeated Sue in a low, earnest voice, before looking down as she gently slid the gold band onto Lucy's finger, leaving the faintest of muddy streaks. It was the perfect fit.

CHAPTER 13

SUE

*S*ue lifted the edge of the heavy curtain and peeped out through the small gap across the grounds of Bamton Hall. It was just getting light, but the whole world seemed to be snoozing under its thick blanket of snow. Everything was peaceful and still.

She let the curtain drop and padded back towards the huge, canopied bed where Lucy was still fast asleep, cuddled up under the heavy blankets with her curls fanned out across the pillows. Sue's heart leapt at the sight of her beautiful best friend. Her wife. How in the world did she come to be so lucky?'

Lifting the blankets, she carefully slid back into the warmth of the bed before propping her head on her hand and gazing down at Lucy's peaceful face. She'd let her sleep. There was no rush, nothing to worry about and nothing urgent to attend to. This morning was theirs to spend as they wished, and if that meant she got to lie here and stare down at Lucy's face as she slept - well, there was nothing in the world that she'd rather be doing right now. Sue gently reached out and stroked a curl away from Lucy's cheek before dropping a soft kiss onto her temple.

Yesterday had been the most magical day of her life. Considering she'd woken up in the morning so full of fear, anxiety and sadness, the magic that had followed had changed her life forever. Their lives forever, she should say. Every single little thing that could have spelt disaster had actually just led to the day becoming more and more special by the second.

First, there was the discovery that Will had secretly been learning to play the guitar ever since he'd arrived at Bamton Hall in the Autumn and had perfected Lucy's favourite in time for the big day. Then there was young Davy, who'd dashed around taking photographs of everyone. He'd even managed to get a sneaky one of her mum's ring still on the carrot before she'd snapped it in half.

They'd spent a very special hour with him out in the snowy grounds after the ceremony, having so much fun that they'd both quickly forgotten to be self-conscious as he captured their special day for them. Sue had a feeling Davy's path in life had changed yesterday too - and from the look of the handful of shots he'd already pinged through to her phone, he was going to have a very long, glittering career in front of him.

Lucy had been exhausted by the time they'd finally dropped into bed the night before, but they'd lain there sharing special moments from the day for hours. She'd finally been able to share every moment of her trip down to the allotments, and Lucy had had tears in her eyes as Sue presented her with one of the two lucky pennies that the detectorists had found there. Eventually, they'd drifted off, wrapped in each other's arms.

Sue glanced down at her hand, admiring the wide hammered white-gold band Lucy had placed there the day before. The single sapphire she'd had set into it mirrored the ruby that nestled in her own. Another little sign that the magic they'd both felt yesterday had been at work for them for far longer than they could even imagine.

Her mind flew briefly back to the little robin she'd spotted on the library windowsill as she'd waited for her bride to arrive. She'd never doubt again that her parents were anywhere other than a heartbeat away, watching over their lives together.

'Your feet are cold,' mumbled Lucy, wriggling under the covers without opening her eyes.

Sue grinned and, wrapping her arms around her, drew Lucy into a huge hug.

'Oh my God,' squealed Lucy, laughing, her eyes flying open, 'you're freezing.'

'Not for long,' chuckled Sue, snuggling against her and earning herself an elbow in the ribs, making her laugh harder. 'I hate to tell you this, but your wifely duties definitely extend to warming my freezing cold feet, my love,' she teased.

'In your dreams,' sighed Lucy, giving up the struggle and settling into Sue's arms.

It lasted all of two seconds before she sat bolt upright, letting a cold blast of air waft under the covers.

'What time is it?' she demanded.

'No idea,' said Sue in surprise. She sat up reluctantly. Why did she suddenly get the feeling that she was going to have a battle on her hands in trying to get Lucy to kick back and relax even for a few hours?

'But it's Christmas Eve!' squeaked Lucy. 'There's so much to do! I haven't even made a start on the sprouts for tomorrow, and there's mulled wine to make for the tree lighting tonight, and mince pies, and-'

'And breathe!' laughed Sue. 'I don't know what time it is - but it's only just getting light!'

She watched as Lucy slumped slightly. 'Oh. Okay, good,' she said, shooting a slightly sheepish grin at Sue.

'And anyway,' said Sue, 'Alf's not going to be back with Thor to pick us up until mid-day. We've got all morning to ourselves.'

'But-!'

'There'll be plenty of time to get everything done this afternoon,' said Sue, wrapping an arm around

Lucy's shoulders. 'Besides, I wouldn't be surprised if we find that Santa's little helpers have been busy by the time we get back down there, anyway.'

'Then we've got to go and help!' said Lucy.

'Nope,' said Sue, 'Little Bamton can wait for once. This morning belongs to us.'

Lucy turned to her, and Sue watched as her expression softened into a smile.

'I love you, wife,' said Lucy, leaning forward and kissing her gently.

'I love you too,' sighed Sue, gathering Lucy to her and snuggling back into the pillows. Sue nuzzled at Lucy's curls, which were ticking her face, and kissed the top of her head. Surely this, right here, was what heaven felt like.

LUCY

'Thank you beautiful boy!' said Lucy, wrapping her hands around Thor's neck and giving him a hug as he crunched happily on a polo.

'Don't I get one of those?' chuckled Alf from behind her.

Lucy smiled and turned to him. 'What? A polo or a hug?'

'Hug please,' he grinned at her, holding his arms out

wide. Lucy gave Thor a quick kiss on the nose and then turned to hug Alf.

'Thank you for everything,' she whispered gratefully in his ear.

'Pleasure was all mine,' said Alf, giving her a bristly kiss on the cheek. 'Erm . . . is yer ma planning on coming to the tree lighting later?' he asked, finally pulling back.

Lucy raised an eyebrow. 'Oh yes. But I think she'll be in the pub with us most of the afternoon . . . if you wanted to spend a bit of time . . . getting to know her?' she added, doing her best to look innocent and failing miserably.

'Smooth,' laughed Sue as she stood waiting to lead Lucy into the pub for the first time as a married couple.

'Smooth or not - I'll be there,' chuckled Alf. 'I'll just get Thor home for his snack and I'll see you girls later.'

Lucy watched as Sue gave Alf a one-armed hug and then patted Thor's neck as Alf climbed back up into his seat. Sue came to stand next to her and the pair of them watched, hand in hand, as the little horse jogged back out of the village square.

'Right,' said Lucy with a huge sigh, 'lots to do. We'd better get in there . . . those sprouts won't prepare themselves!'

She took one step towards the door, but Sue tugged on her hand pulling her back close.

'One sec, my love,' said Sue, steadying her as she

slipped slightly on the thick, powdery snow that lay at their feet.

Lucy's knees went weak as Sue leaned in and gently kissed her lips. The heat of the contact ran through her, warming her all the way from her chilly cheeks to her toes, which still felt frozen from their carriage ride down from the hall.

Lucy smiled at Sue as she pulled back. 'What?' she said, catching her eye.

'Thank you,' said Sue.

'What for?' laughed Lucy, stamping her feet in a bid to stop them from turning into little blocks of ice.

'For marrying me,' said Sue, a huge smile spreading over her face.

'Oh, you sappy mare,' laughed Lucy, stepping forward and kissing her again.

'Oi! You two love birds!'

The shout from the doorway of the pub made them both jump, their heads whipping around to see who it was.

'Horace!' laughed Lucy, shaking her head.

'Are you coming in, or are you going to canoodle out there in the snow until it's time for the tree-lighting?'

'What do you reckon?' asked Sue, turning to look at Lucy with a grin on her face.

'Well . . . I *could* murder a hot chocolate,' laughed Lucy.

'In that case . . . give me one sec!'

Lucy watched in confusion as Sue strode over to Horace and handed him the bag she was carrying. Then she walked back to Lucy and, dropping a quick kiss on her cheek, scooped her right off her feet.

Lucy let out a squeal of surprise and threw her arms around Sue's neck, holding on for dear life. 'You complete nutcase,' she giggled as Sue navigated her way across the patch of snow towards the open pub door.

With some difficulty and a funny little sideways, ducking action, Sue managed to manoeuvre the pair of them through the doorway and into the warmth of the bar without bashing either of them on the head while she was at it.

They were greeted by a round of cheers and clapping, and as her eyes adjusted to the golden glow, Lucy realised that they were surrounded by all their friends. She couldn't stop giggling as Sue set her down safely and kissed her on the cheek.

'So romantic!' sighed Scarlet from her perch over near the fireplace.

'Soppy buggers,' muttered Davy who was sitting across from her. Lucy grinned over at them, noticing a huge pile of sprout peelings between them and a couple of discarded knives lying on the table.

'Christmas elves!' she said, turning to Sue.

'See - I told you there was no reason to worry,' laughed Sue.

'Well,' said Lucy as a little buzz of energy ran through her, 'there's still the stuffing, the potatoes, the carrots, the . . .' she trailed off. Sue was shaking her head from side to side as she listed each item on her Christmas to-do list. 'What do you mean "no"?' demanded Lucy.

'She means - done, done and . . . done!' chuckled Violet from her spot behind the bar.

'We've been here all morning,' said Finn, striding out from the little kitchen at the back with Wilf the Westie trotting at his heels. Finn was wearing one of her flowery aprons and had his shirt sleeves rolled up to his elbows.

'Yep,' nodded Caro, from where she was sitting with Amber, Will, Sam, Emmy and Jon. By the look of the heap of peelings on their table, they'd been on potato duty.

'Okay - so that leaves me the mince pies, then?' said Lucy as she felt Sue's arms snake around her waist.

'Did someone ask for a mince pie?' said Eve, appearing from the kitchen with a plate piled high.

'Oh for goodness sake!' said Lucy, as everyone started to laugh.

'Happy?' Sue whispered in her ear.

Lucy smiled at her over her shoulder and nodded - then went completely still.

'What is it?' asked Horace, raising his eyebrows.

'I'd better get the mulled wine on,' said Lucy, triumphantly.

'No need,' he said. 'Where do you think your mum is right now?!'

✳

'Every year we come here, and every year the message is the same.'

Mark's gentle voice travelled across the darkened churchyard, and Lucy threaded the fingers of her free hand through Sue's as she listened to the words that were just as powerful now as they were all those years ago when she'd first heard them.

'Let the light of Christmas kindle inside you. Let it catch in your hearts and warm your own homes first. That way, it will shine out and bless all those around you, making our village, our country, and the rest of the world a more special place.'

Lucy watched with tears in her eyes as Mark held out his candle, and the young lad who was bearing this year's Christmas flame lit it for him. Before long, candles were being lit all around them, the light spreading, lifting the darkness.

'Here, Luce,' said Sue gently, turning to her with her own lit candle. She cupped the flame as Lucy leaned in and lit her own from it.

'I love you,' Lucy whispered, her eyes locked on Sue's as the candlelight flickered in their depths.

'I love you too,' said Sue, with a soft smile.

'Who thinks it's time to light the tree?' called Mark's voice from the front.

A huge cheer went up all around them, and they threw their voices into the mix.

'Three!'

'Two!'

'One!'

Suddenly, the Christmas tree and the whole of Little Bamton was bathed in twinkling, magical light.

THE END

ALSO BY BETH RAIN

Little Bamton Series:

Little Bamton: The Complete Series Collection: Books 1 - 5

Individual titles:

Christmas Lights and Snowball Fights (Little Bamton Book 1)

Spring Flowers and April Showers (Little Bamton Book 2)

Summer Nights and Pillow Fights (Little Bamton Book 3)

Autumn Cuddles and Muddy Puddles (Little Bamton Book 4)

Christmas Flings and Wedding Rings (Little Bamton Book 5)

Upper Bamton Series:

A New Arrival in Upper Bamton (Upper Bamton Book 1)

Rainy Days in Upper Bamton (Upper Bamton Book 2)

Hidden Treasures in Upper Bamton (Upper Bamton Book 3)

Time Flies By in Upper Bamton (Upper Bamton Book 4)

Standalone Books:

Christmas on Crumcarey

Seabury Series:

Welcome to Seabury (Seabury Book 1)

Trouble in Seabury (Seabury Book 2)

Christmas in Seabury (Seabury Book 3)

Sandwiches in Seabury (Seabury Book 4)

Secrets in Seabury (Seabury Book 5)

Surprises in Seabury (Seabury Book 6)

Dreams and Ice Creams in Seabury (Seabury Book 7)

Mistakes and Heartbreaks in Seabury (Seabury Book 8)

Laughter and Happy Ever After in Seabury (Seabury Book 9)

Seabury Series Collections:

Kate's Story: Books 1 - 3

Hattie's Story: Books 4 - 6

Writing as Bea Fox:

What's a Girl To Do? The Complete Series

Individual titles:

The Holiday: What's a Girl To Do? (Book 1)

The Wedding: What's a Girl To Do? (Book 2)

The Lookalike: What's a Girl To Do? (Book 3)

The Reunion: What's a Girl To Do? (Book 4)

At Christmas: What's a Girl To Do? (Book 5)

ABOUT THE AUTHOR

Beth Rain has always wanted to be a writer and has been penning adventures for characters ever since she learned to stare into the middle-distance and daydream.

She currently lives in the (sometimes) sunny South West, and it is a dream come true to spend her days hanging out with Bob – her trusty laptop – scoffing crisps and chocolate while dreaming up swoony love stories for all her imaginary friends.

Beth's writing will always deliver on the happy-ever-afters, so if you need cosy… you're in safe hands!

Visit www.bethrain.com for all the bookish goodness and keep up with all Beth's news by joining her monthly newsletter!

facebook.com/BethRainBooks
twitter.com/bethrainauthor
instagram.com/bethrainauthor

Printed in Great Britain
by Amazon